# Journeys Within

## Stories

### Don Tassone

Copyright © 2024 Don Tassone
ISBN: 978-93-95131-65-0

First Edition: 2024
Rs. 500/-

ROCHAK PUBLISHING
HIG 45 Kaushambi Kunj, Kalindipuram
Allahabad - 211011 (U.P.) India
http://www.cyberwit.net
E-mail: info@rochakpublishing.com

No part of this book may be reproduced or transmitted in any form or by any means, electronic, mechanical, photocopying, or otherwise, without the express written consent of Don Tassone.

Printed at Repro India Limited.

**For Liz**

# Contents

## Stories

| | |
|---|---|
| The Hope | 8 |
| Book Covers | 22 |
| Down in the Valley | 30 |
| The Secret Bookshelf | 40 |
| Time to Choose | 50 |
| The Architect | 57 |
| Conversation on a Park Bench | 69 |
| How to Get Promoted | 80 |
| Filling Gaps | 85 |
| Lost and Found | 95 |
| The Bargain | 107 |
| Reset | 114 |
| A Final Message | 128 |
| Bully | 137 |
| Bare Essence | 153 |
| Calling | 165 |
| The Adoption | 174 |
| Refuge | 180 |
| The Apostle | 188 |
| Long Way Home | 207 |

## Flash Fiction

| | |
|---|---|
| Grow | 222 |
| The Secret | 226 |
| Unintentional | 229 |
| The Fault, Dear Brutus | 231 |
| The Conversation | 235 |

| | |
|---|---|
| The Garden | 239 |
| See for Yourself | 240 |
| Perfect Communion | 243 |
| History Lesson | 245 |
| Play | 249 |

# Preface

"The only journey is the one within," wrote the Austrian poet and novelist Rainer Maria Rilke.

The characters in many of the stories in this collection are on such journeys. Unexpected events prompt them to take a fresh look at their lives and their choices. What they discover sets them on a new path.

This collection features an eclectic mix of 30 stories. I hope you enjoy them all.

Don Tassone
March 2024

**Stories**

## The Hope

Growing up near Gaza, Gabe often woke up to explosions and was lulled to sleep by music. The former nearly broke him. The latter surely saved him.

Gabe lived with his parents and two sisters in a small house made of stone. His father worked in the textile business. His family lived modestly. Their house had two bedrooms. Gabe's parents shared one. His sisters shared the other. Gabe slept on the sofa.

He was a sensitive boy. When bombs rocked his house or gunfire pierced the air, Gabe would crawl into bed with his parents, shaking and crying.

His parents talked about moving. But no place in Israel was free of violence in those days, and they couldn't afford to move anyway.

Gabe walked to school with his sisters and other kids from the neighborhood. There were no school buses. Parents hoped that, by staying together, their children would somehow be safe walking to and from school.

But the sounds of explosions, even when he was ensconced within the high stone walls of his school, affected Gabe deeply. He couldn't concentrate. He often cried, though he tried to hide his tears. His grades suffered.

The only thing that calmed him was a sound that began in the early evening nearly every day. It was the sweet, soft, soulful sound of a violin being played by someone near Gabe's house.

Whenever he heard it, Gabe closed his eyes. He was entranced by the music. It carried him away, away from the violence of the day, into the stillness of the night. Only then did he feel at peace. Only then was he unafraid.

"Where is that music coming from?" he asked his mother.

"Oh, that is old Mr. Rueben," she said. "He does play the violin beautifully, doesn't he?"

"I've never heard anything like it."

"Would you like to visit him sometime?"

"I'd love that!"

"Well, I'm sure he would too. I've known Mr. Rueben for years. He's a very kind man. Actually, you've seen him. He's a baker. We buy bread in his bakery."

"Oh, yeah."

"I'll see Mr. Rueben in the morning. I'll ask if we can pay him a visit some evening, so you can listen to him play. Would you like that?"

"I'd love it."

That night, Gabe fell asleep to the sound of Rueben's violin. He dreamed of being lifted up by the music, of the music carrying him across the sky. In his dream, he could still hear explosions down below, but they were muted by the dulcet tones of a violin.

Gabe slept soundly that night. In the morning, for the first time in a long time, he woke up feeling happy.

"Well, hello, Mrs. Schwartz," Rueben said, standing in his doorway, smiling at Gabe's mother and looking down at the boy holding her hand. "And you must be Gabe."

Rueben was a small man with an easy smile. His hair was thin and white, his beard neatly trimmed. He wore a loose-fitting white shirt, baggy olive pants and brown sandals.

"Good evening, Mr. Rueben," Gabe's mother said. "Yes, this is my son, Gabriel. He's been in your bakery, but I don't think you two have met. Gabe, this is Mr. Rueben."

"I'm very pleased to meet you, young man," Rueben said. "I've heard you like violin music."

"Yes," Gabe said, feeling nervous.

"Well," the old man said with a smile, "you've come to the right place because it just so happens I *play* the violin."

"I know," Gabe said. "I hear you every evening."

"You do? Well, would you like to come in and allow me to play something for you?"

"Yes," Gabe said, looking up at his mother and smiling.

Rueben led them into his spacious living room. The plaster walls were white and adorned with paintings of the sea. A Persian rug covered much of the tiled floor. A plate of cheese, fruit and bread had been set upon a coffee table next to the sofa.

"Please," he said, "help yourselves. Would you like something to drink? I have juice or, if you like, wine."

"Some juice would be very nice," Gabe's mother said.

"I'll be right back."

Gabe sat next to his mother on the sofa. He spotted a black violin case on a wooden bench in the corner. His heart raced. Soon Rueben returned with two glasses of grape juice.

"Thank you, Mr. Rueben," Gabe's mother said.

"Thank you," said Gabe.

"My pleasure. Now, while you enjoy some refreshment, let me play for you."

Rueben stepped over the to violin case, unlatched it and carefully lifted out a burgundy-colored violin and a black bow. He placed the case on the floor and sat down on the bench. He looked at his guests and smiled.

Then he tucked the end of the violin under his chin, raised the bow and closed his eyes. With his fingers pressed on the strings, he slowly drew the bow across the instrument, and Gabe heard a sound he had heard only in the distance. Now it reverberated within the walls of the room. He had never heard anything like it — or felt anything like it. It was as if the sound were resonating within him.

Gabe was so moved that he began to cry. Listening to the music, he felt transported, just as he had in his dream.

When the last note faded away and the room was silent, Gabe became conscious of his tears. Embarrassed, he wiped them away.

"I'm sorry," he said.

"Please don't be sorry," Rueben said. "You honor me with your heartfelt emotion."

After that, Gabe began walking over the Rueben's house in the evening on his own. He would sit and listen to Rueben play, mesmerized by the music.

Rueben seemed to enjoy having an audience. One evening, he asked Gabe if he would like to learn to play the violin.

"I'd love to," he said.

"Well, I would be happy to teach you. There's only one thing."

"What's that?"

"You need a violin."

"I'll ask my parents."

"New violins can be expensive. There's a music store in town where you might be able to buy a used one. If money's a problem, maybe I could help out."

"Thank you. I'll let my parents know."

Gabe went home and asked his parents. They shot each other worried looks.

"We'll see what we can do," his father said.

"Mr. Rueben said he might be able to help," Gabe said.

"Well, that's very generous. But let us see what's out there and what we might be able to afford."

A few days later, Gabe came home from school and, as usual, did his homework at the kitchen table. He looked over at a cabinet where his mother kept her china dinnerware, a wedding gift. Now, though, the shelf where it had always been was empty.

"Mami, where is your china?" Gabe said, pointing to the cabinet.

His mother came over and took his hand.

"Gabe, Abba found a very nice violin for you in town. To pay for it, he sold our china. He'll be bringing it home tonight. We wanted it to be a surprise, but I think you should know."

Gabe was stunned. He knew his mother loved that china. He'd seen her handle it with great care on the high holidays and other special occasions when she set it out.

"No, Mami! You shouldn't have sold your china."

"Gabe, I have never seen you so happy as when Mr. Rueben played his violin for you. That music is the only thing that seems to bring you peace. Abba and I want you to be happy. We are happy to do this for you."

Gabe was so moved that he began to cry. His mother embraced him, and he held her tight.

That evening, Gabe's father came home carrying a violin case. Gabe ran to him and hugged him.

"Thank you, Abba."

His father looked over at his mother.

"I told him," she said with a smile. "It's okay."

After dinner, Gabe sat and held his new violin. It was burgundy, like Rueben's. It was the most beautiful thing Gabe had ever seen. He sat staring at it, checking out every part of it, gently running his fingers along the strings, down the fingerboard, over the body.

Finally, he carefully put it back in its case, which he placed on the coffee table next to the sofa. He lay gazing at it in the dim light until he fell asleep.

The following evening, Gabe brought his violin with him to Rueben's house.

"Oh, my! What have we here?"

"My parents bought me a violin," Gabe said, beaming.

"Come in, and let's take a look."

They went into the living room. Gabe laid his violin on the coffee table and opened the case.

"Wow!" Rueben said. "What a beauty!"

"It looks like yours."

"It does indeed."

"Will you teach me to play?"

"Nothing could bring me more joy."

Then Rueben began what would become years of instruction. He taught Gabe how to read music, how to hold the violin, how to press the strings, how to work the bow. He introduced him to both classical pieces and contemporary songs.

Gabe learned quickly, and he had a knack for the violin. By the time he was 12, he was playing nearly as well as Rueben, and his lesson time had turned into playing time for the two of them.

Along the way, Rueben and Gabe got to know each other. They shared their stories.

Rueben was born in Romania. His parents were Holocaust survivors. They moved to Israel when the country was established and Rueben was a young boy. He learned to play the violin from his father, who was a classically trained musician.

"He told me the thing he missed most in the camps was the sound of music," Rueben said. "I think that's why he played so much and taught me to play. He wanted his music to live on."

When he was a young man, Rueben married a beautiful young woman named Rachael. They had no children. Still, they lived together happily until she died, around the time Gabe was born. Rueben had lived alone ever since.

"So why do you still play the violin?" Gabe asked him once.

"I play for the same reason I bake bread," he said. "Bread and music are both important. One nourishes the body. The other nourishes the soul. Baking bread and playing music, doing both, makes me feel whole."

Gabe smiled. Rueben had a way of explaining things that Gabe could understand.

"And what about you?" Rueben said. "Why do you play the violin?"

"When I was little, the sound of bombs and gunfire terrified me. But in the evening, the sound of your violin soothed me. Your music reminded me there is still something beautiful in the world. I wanted to bring that kind of comfort and beauty into the world too."

Rueben smiled and nodded.

"I believe the whole world will one day be moved by your music," he said.

On one of the first days of music class in high school, Gabe played his violin for his teacher. She was astonished by his proficiency.

"I think you could play with the Young Israel Philharmonic Orchestra," she said.

"What's that?"

"It's a group of our country's best young players of orchestral instruments. I know someone there. Would you like me to see if I can get you an audition?"

"Sure."

A few weeks later, she drove him to Tel Aviv, less than an hour away, to audition in the theater where the junior orchestra performed. Gabe played for the conductor himself. He played the first movement from Mendelssohn's Violin Concerto, a piece he had practiced many times with Rueben.

When he was finished, the conductor just sat there, saying nothing, looking stunned. Gabe wasn't sure what to think. Then the man stood and began to clap.

"Bravo!" he said. "Young Mr. Schwartz, we will find a place for you here."

Gabe was thrilled. One evening, six months later, the conductor called Gabe to tell him he had been chosen to join the orchestra that summer. He would fill the vacancy created by a violinist who had turned 18 and would be leaving the program.

Gabe's mother drove him to rehearsals that summer. From the start, Gabe impressed everyone with his mastery of the violin. But he had a lot to learn too. Other than Rueben, he had never played music with anyone else. Learning how to blend with so many other musicians was a challenge for Gabe. But by the end of that summer, he played his parts seamlessly.

He also got to know 99 other teenagers from all over Israel. Until then, Gabe hadn't left his small town. Meeting other young people from very different places and backgrounds expanded Gabe. And traveling to Tel Aviv, Jerusalem and Haifa for concerts gave him a glimpse of a larger world.

Gabe was now playing with his country's most talented young musicians. But even among this elite group, he stood out. Seeing his extraordinary talent and promise, the conductor named Gabe first chair violinist in just his second year. At just 16, Gabe was leading the orchestra in tuning before concerts and rehearsals.

The conductor also let Gabe stand next to him and play a prominent violin part in a piece by Tchaikovsky just before intermission at each concert.

At first, Gabe was nervous and a bit stiff. But in time, he moved fluidly, his body rising and swaying with the music, his long hair whipping around his head, his violin bobbing and weaving. The audience loved it. Gabe got a standing ovation every time.

Rueben came to see the youth orchestra perform in Jerusalem. Gabe had arranged for him to sit in the front row. His eyes were fixed on Gabe the whole time. Several times, he was overcome by emotion and wept. Seeing this, Gabe kept his eyes on his sheet music lest he break down too.

Gabe was becoming a star. In its reviews of the orchestra, *The Jerusalem Times* called him a "prodigy." Videos of Gabe performing became YouTube sensations. And all of this was happening while he was still in high school, where he'd become very popular, especially with the girls.

The violin had been calling to Gabe all is life, and he was answering the call. By his senior year in high school, Gabe knew he would be a professional musician.

First, though, he would have to join the Israeli military for 32 months, a requirement of every 18-year-old in Israel.

When he showed up for duty, Gabe told the officer in charge he was opposed to war but wanted to serve by entertaining the troops.

The officer looked up at him and scoffed.

Undaunted, Gabe said, "May I play something for you?"

He'd brought his violin with him. The officer sat back in his chair, folded his arms and nodded.

Gabe opened his case, took out his violin and began playing "Hatikvah," the Israeli national anthem.

The officer looked astonished. When Gabe was finished, he looked around the room and saw all the other conscripts standing at attention.

"Okay," he said. "I'll get you into one of our ensembles."

For the next two and a half years, Gabe performed with a group of 10 musicians and singers. They toured the nearly 70 military bases throughout Israel. Each of their shows concluded with a soaring rendition of Hatikvah, which means "The Hope."

This experience too expanded Gabe. He not only got to see all of Israel, he was exposed to the personal stories of those who had defended his homeland. They didn't change his opposition to war, but they helped him more fully appreciate the sacrifice others had made on his behalf.

Not that the conflict had ever gone away. Whenever he went, Gabe heard explosions and gunfire. It reminded him of the sounds of violence that had so frightened him as a young boy. But now it was he who, like Rueben, was bringing a measure of peace.

Finally, when his military service was over, Gabe was able to study music. He knew he needed a degree to play with the Israel Philharmonic Orchestra, and that was now his goal.

With his talent and experience, Gabe had his pick of schools in Israel. He chose The Buchmann-Mehta School of Music because he qualified for a full scholarship and would have the opportunity to study under the Israel Philharmonic.

At 21, he moved to Tel Aviv and began his study. Students at Buchmann-Mehta came from all over the world. This further expanded Gabe.

One student in particular really caught his eye. Her name was Ania. Blue-eyed, blond and petite, she hailed from Warsaw and played the harp. To Gabe, she looked like an angel.

After music history class one day, he asked her to have coffee. She said yes. They clicked immediately, began dating and fell in love.

It was one of the best things that had ever happened to Gabe. One of the worst occurred during his junior year, when he got a call from his mother.

"Gabe, I am so sorry to tell you this," she said, her voice breaking. "Mr. Rueben has died."

Gabe maintained his composure while he was on the phone. But as soon as he hung up, he sat down and wept for a long time.

Then he wiped away his tears, picked up his violin and thought of a song Rueben had taught him, "Amazing Grace."

"Isn't that a Christian song?" Gabe had said at the time.

"Maybe so," Rueben said. "But it's about a man who was saved by God's grace. I have been saved by God's grace. This song speaks to me. Plus, it's so beautiful. Let's play it together, shall we?"

Now Gabe raised his bow and began to slowly, reverently play "Amazing Grace." He imagined playing it with Mr. Rueben. He could well imagine that because Mr. Rueben had saved him.

Upon graduation, Gabe realized his dream and joined the Israel Philharmonic Orchestra. Just as he had with the junior orchestra, he stood out.

However, he was no longer called a prodigy. Now Gabe was becoming known as a virtuoso. Soon he began receiving invitations to perform as a guest violinist with symphony orchestras all over the world.

And now that he finally had an income, he asked Ania to marry him. Happily, she said yes. They were married in Tel Aviv, where they bought a small house and started a family.

Gabe was playing with the Vienna Philharmonic when Hamas attacked Israel. Hearing the news, he immediately called Ania to make sure she and their children were safe. Thankfully, they were.

"But I'm worried about your parents," she said.

Gabe then called his parents' house. They were still living in the same house near Gaza, his boyhood home.

He was relieved when his mother answered.

"It's awful," she said. "We are afraid."

"Mami, stay where you are. I'm going to have someone come there and pick you and Abba up and bring you to Tel Aviv. You can live with us until it's safe for you to return home."

Gabe arranged for his parents to be driven to his house the following morning. Then he rushed to the airport in Vienna and took the next flight to Tel Aviv.

He thought about moving his family, and now his parents, to a safer location. But where? He knew the Israeli army was already beginning to mobilize for a counterattack and that Tel Aviv would now be well protected. Who knew if nearby countries would be any safer?

So Gabe decided to stay put. He had the orchestra postpone his scheduled guest appearances with other orchestras around the world. They all understood.

Early one morning, Gabe awoke to the sound of an explosion in the distance. He was shaking. He thought about all the missiles now being fired into Gaza and the West Bank. He thought about how terrified the people there must be.

He eyed his violin case on a table in the corner. He thought of Mr. Rueben and how his music had saved him as a boy. He wondered how different his life might have turned out if Mr. Rueben had not chosen to share his gift.

"You're going where?" Ania said with a look of disbelief.

"I must go," Gabe said, holding her hands. "I can get there in an hour, and I'll be back tonight in time to put the kids to bed."

"But you won't be safe."

"I'll be fine. The shelling is now within Gaza. The border is fortified."

"But Gabe, why? Why must you do this?"

"Ania, I would not be here today were it not for music, music that gave me comfort and hope as a boy. This is what the people of Gaza need most right now. Being able to play the violin is my gift. I have to share it. I have to share it with people who need to know there is still beauty in the world."

Ania embraced her husband and held him for a long time, knowing she could not keep him from what he saw as a sacred task.

That afternoon, Gabe drove 40 miles southwest to the outskirts of Gaza, not far from his parents' house. He took his violin and bow from his case and, as the sun began to set over Gaza, he began to play. He continued playing as darkness fell and the sound of explosions in the distance began to taper off. Then he drove home.

Gabe did this all along the border of Gaza, day after day, night after night, until the war was over. He stood there alone and created in the midst of destruction.

Sometimes, Israelis would gather to hear him play. Sometimes Palestinians across the border would gather too. His music, of course, knew no border. It reached them all the same.

## Book Covers

Cassidy had just finished taking yet another complex coffee order when he caught her eye as he walked in. He was tall, with long, brown, tousled hair, heavy stubble, a form-fitting t-shirt, tight jeans, rugged boots and an athletic build. As he strode over to get in line, she could not take her eyes off him.

She and her girlfriends had made a pact. They would date only guys of depth. They'd all been burned by nice-looking guys who had no substance or, worse, turned out to be jerks.

And Cassidy still remembered her mother's advice from the time she was a girl: "Watch out for pretty boys."

Cassidy had followed that advice. Now, though, as this gorgeous guy got closer and she noticed he wasn't wearing a ring, Cassidy thought it might be time to make an exception.

She smiled at him as he got in line. He looked her way and smiled back. He had a pleasant smile. Surely his personality must match, she thought.

Now he stood right in front of her.

"Good morning," she said.

"Good morning."

He was even better-looking up close. His eyes were blue, his jawline was strong and his arms were toned.

"May I help you?" she said.

"Yes, just a small black coffee with a little room for cream," he said, making eye contact.

Somehow she knew his order would be simple and elegant.

"Will that be for here or to go?" she said, hoping he'd be sticking around.

"For here," he said.

Her heart fluttered.

"Very good," she said. "That'll be $2.75."

He pulled out his wallet and handed her a five. Cash. Old-fashioned guy, she thought.

"Please keep the change," he said with a smile.

His teeth were straight and dazzling white.

"Thank you very much," she said. "If you like, I can bring you your coffee when it's ready."

"That'd be great. Thank you."

"May I have a name for your order?"

"Sure. It's Alex."

What a strong name, she thought. It fits.

"Okay, Alex," she said. "I'll be over shortly."

"Thanks."

He stepped away, sat down at a table for two and opened a book.

The shop's protocol was to call customers' names when their orders were ready so they could pick them up. But Cassidy wanted to make a personal connection in this case. So she had a co-worker cover for her while she made Alex's coffee and brought it over.

"Here you are," she said, setting his coffee mug in front of him. "You said room for cream. Would you like some?"

He gave her a curious look.

"I can get it, miss. But thank you."

He stood up. This close, he seemed even taller.

"Okay," she said. "But if you need anything else, just let me know. My name is Cassidy."

He looked down at her name tag.

"Thank you, Cassidy."

She liked hearing him say her name.

She followed him over to the cream and sugar station. He looked good from the back too. Then she slipped behind the counter, where she resumed taking orders and watching him.

It wasn't just good-looking guys Cassidy was cautious around. It was guys in general. Cassidy was beautiful, blond and shapely, and she'd learned how superficial guys could be. She hoped this one wasn't being nice just because of her looks, even though she was acting like a school girl because of his.

She snatched glimpses of him drinking his coffee and reading his book. She liked how he took his time, sipping his coffee, engrossed in his book. She liked the blue-green color of the cover, but she couldn't see the title. She wondered what he liked to read.

After a little while, he tilted his coffee mug all the way back. He's finished, she thought. Maybe he'd like a refill. Not wasting any time, she grabbed a pot, poured in some black coffee and went over to his table.

"Would you care for a refill?" she said.

He looked up.

"Wow," he said with a smile. "You're full service. Sure, I'd love some."

He slid his mug over.

"Room for cream?" she said.

"Yes, please."

Please. He's polite too, she thought.

"Thank you," he said.

"May I get you anything else?"

"No, thank you, Cassidy."

*He remembered my name!*

From behind the counter, she continued to watch him. Finally, he got up, walked over to the cream and sugar station and deposited his mug.

*Oh, no. He's leaving.*

But he stopped and turned back toward the counter. Seeing Cassidy there, he smiled and gave her a little wave.

She waved back. Then he turned around and left, and Cassidy wondered if she would ever see him again.

The rest of that day, she couldn't stop thinking of him. The following day, she kept looking for him, but he didn't show. The day after that, she began to lose hope. She had just grabbed an order for a Cafe Americano when she turned around, and he was there, waiting in line.

He smiled at her. Her knees felt weak.

"Good morning, Cassidy," he said.

*He remembered my name!*

"Good morning," she said, unable to remember his name in the excitement of the moment.

He looked different. He'd swapped out his t-shirt and jeans for a polo and khakis, his hair was neatly combed and he was clean-shaven. *Good Lord! He looks like a model.*

By the time he reached her, she remembered his name.

"How you are today, Alex?"

"I'm doing well. It's good to see you again."

She wondered if he meant that or if it was a standard line. But then, looking up into his blue eyes, she decided to believe him.

"And you," she said. "What can I get started for you?"

"I'll have a black coffee for here, please, with room for cream."

"You've got it. That'll be $2.75."

Again, he handed her a five and told her to keep the change.

"I'll have that out to you in just a couple of minutes," she said.

"Thank you," he said with a smile.

Once again, she watched him sit down and open a book. A few minutes later, she brought his coffee over. This time, though, she had added some cream and slipped a spoon into his mug.

"I went ahead and added cream," she said, setting his mug on the table. "I hope it's to your liking."

"Thank you. I'm sure it will be."

She noticed the title of his book, *All the Light We Cannot See*.

"I've heard that's good," she said.

"Yes, it's quite good."

"Is it a novel?"

"Yeah, an historical novel."

"Ah."

"Do you enjoy reading?" he said.

"Oh, yeah. Writing too."

"Are you a writer?"

"I love to write, but I've never been published."

"I'd love to try my hand at writing," he said.

"Why don't you?"

"I don't know. Too busy, I guess."

"Well, they say every good writer must first be a great reader," she said.

He looked at her and smiled.

"Cassidy, I hope this won't seem too forward, but would you like to have dinner sometime?"

Her heart skipped a beat.

"Sure."

That Saturday, they met at 6:00 at an Italian restaurant near the coffee shop. He'd made a reservation.

It was a hot summer evening. She wore a white sundress. He wore a white short-sleeved shirt and olive khakis. He was already there when she arrived.

"Hello, Cassidy," he said, getting up when she walked in. "You look beautiful."

*Beautiful.* She had been called that many times in her life. She had learned to be suspicious. This time, though, she decided to take the compliment. After all, until then, Alex had only ever seen her in a barista uniform with her hair pulled back.

"Thank you," she said. "You look very nice too."

"Thanks. Our table is ready, if you'd like to sit down."

"Sure."

When they were seated, he said, "By the way, my last name is Harrison."

"Alex Harrison," she said. "That has a nice ring to it."

"Thanks."

"And my last name is McKenna."

"Well, that would explain your red hair," he said. "It's lovely."

*What kind of man uses the word lovely? A man who's confident in his masculinity.*

Their waitress came. They each ordered a glass of red wine.

"So you're a writer," he said.

"Well, I like to write."

"That's cool. What have you written?"

"Short stories and a couple of novels."

"Wow!"

"And you said you'd love to try to your hand at writing," she said.

"Yeah. I'd love to write, but I've never had any training. I'm just not sure where to begin."

"Writing's not so hard," she said. "You just have to stick with it. But publishing, now that's the hard part."

"Really? Well, that's the part I know something about."

"You do?"

"Yeah, I work with publishers all the time."

"Really? What kind of work do you do?"

"I design book covers."

"How interesting."

Their waitress brought their wine.

"Would you care to order?" she said.

"We'll need a few minutes," he said.

They raised their glasses.

"To writing," she said.

"And getting published."

They clinked their glasses and looked into one another's eyes.

"So how did you get into designing book covers?" she said.

They talked for hours. They shared their life stories. She offered to be his writing coach, and he offered to get her manuscripts read by the right publishers.

Years later, when they'd both become bestselling authors, they got a sitter for the kids and went to dinner at the restaurant where they'd had their first date.

"Mom warned me about pretty boys like you," she said with a smile.

"Don't you know you should never judge a book by its cover?" he said, leaning across the table and giving her a kiss.

## Down in the Valley

Pulling into his reserved parking space near the entrance of Evo's garage, Chase Asbury smiled. Once again, he had beat his boss, Evo's CEO, and his fellow vice chairmen to the office. When they arrived, they would see his turbocharged Audi R8 and be reminded who was in the lead.

Chase had spent nearly 30 years climbing this corporate ladder. He knew if Jack retired soon, he'd have at least five years to make his mark as Evo's CEO.

Some thought Chase had hung on too long, that he should have left and become CEO somewhere else. But Chase Asbury was devoted to Evo, the only place he'd ever worked. Technically, he was one of three contenders for the top spot. But years earlier, Jack had told Chase privately it was his job to lose.

Chase was taking no chances. He still gave the company everything he had every day. He also took every opportunity to be seen building his part of Evo's business, its large and profitable power tools division. He enjoyed being in the limelight.

Now, flipping the light switch in his corner office on the 49th floor of the Steel Building, Chase hung up his suit coat, stepped over to the window wall behind his mahogany desk and looked out at the twinkling lights of the dark city below. He imagined the lights down in the valley where he'd grown up, near the banks of the Monongahela River, might have looked something like this from the hills of Morgantown before sunrise.

How far I've come, he thought. Just one more step, and I will have reached the summit.

Chase's first job was cutting grass for his neighbors and others in the valley. He charged $5 a yard.

He thought about trying for customers a little closer to town. He knew he could charge them more. But he had to push his mower and carry his gas, and some of those higher-paying jobs would have been a mile or more away. Plus, he was able to line up at least 10 customers in the valley every summer. With tips, he could make $60 a week, very good money for a 12-year-old boy in 1980s Appalachia.

He would never forget the satisfaction of stuffing those bills or sometimes a handful of change into his pocket after pushing and sweating his way through somebody's yard. In those days, Chase knew what five dollars meant. He could feel them in his pocket.

The summer after he turned 16, Chase stopped cutting grass and started working in a hardware/lumber store in Morgantown. He rode his bike and worked there six days a week.

He cleared $150 a week, more than his brothers and friends were making. And although he didn't know it, he was making about a third of what his father was bringing home at the time.

Growing up, Chase and his brothers took turns riding their bikes to the grocery store to buy food and other staples for their mother. She would send them off with a shopping list and $20.

But as Chase began making more money, his mother began asking him, and not his brothers, to go to the store for her.

One day she gave him only a shopping list, no money. Chase didn't realize it until he was checking out. Fortunately, he had his wallet, and he paid for the groceries.

When he got home, his mother didn't say anything about the money. Nor did Chase. From then on, he simply paid for the family's groceries with his own money.

His mother always thanked him, but that's not why Chase did it. He knew his family was living on a shoestring, and he had plenty of money. Buying milk, bread and cereal for his family simply made Chase feel good, and he liked to make his mother happy.

And he still had plenty of money to buy himself nice things, like a new bike and records, as well as save for college. Looking around Morgantown growing up, Chase decided early he would leave for a bigger city and a better life as soon as he could.

After high school, Chase went to nearby West Virginia University, where he majored in finance. Between the scholarships he earned and the money he'd saved, Chase could easily afford it. To save even more money, he lived at home, although he insisted on paying his parents rent. He also took the bus to school because he'd chosen not to buy a car.

Every summer during college, Chase interned at Evo, which was based in Pittsburgh, an hour north of Morgantown. It was too far to commute, so he rented a small apartment in Pittsburgh each summer.

His internships gave him an inside look at how a company operates and a good-sized company at that. Evo was all about work. It made power tools, work equipment and workwear. Morgantown was a blue-collar town, and of course Chase had been working hard for years. So he felt right at home at Evo.

Living in Pittsburgh also gave Chase an appreciation for the amenities of a larger city, from ethnic markets and eateries to museums and parks. It was a different world from the barebones one he'd known, and he knew he wanted to live in a place like this when he got out of school.

The summer after his sophomore year at WVU, Chase met a young woman who was also interning at Evo. Her name was Amy. She was a student at Duquesne and was working in the marketing department. She was pretty and petite. Chase had seen her around the office, but they hadn't met. He introduced himself to her at a get-together for Evo interns one Friday evening.

Chase and Amy hit it off right away and started dating. Beyond being physically attracted to each other, he was drawn to her grace, and she was drawn to his drive.

"I'm going to be CEO of this company one day," he told her.

"I'm sure you will be," she said with a smile.

That fall, Chase bought his first car. It was an old beater but reliable enough to make weekend trips to Pittsburgh to see Amy.

After his third summer interning with Evo, Chase got an offer to join the company after graduation. He would work in the finance department, starting right after graduation.

Amy got an offer from Evo too. But although she liked the work she'd done during her internships, the corporate environment just didn't suit her, so she declined. After graduation, she took a job with an advertising agency in Pittsburgh.

A year after they graduated, Chase and Amy got engaged. A year later, they were married.

Living with Chase, Amy began to understand just how driven Chase was. Most days, he was in the office early and stayed late. He missed dinner a lot. He worked on weekends too.

Amy wanted to be supportive of Chase's career, but she wanted to spend time with him too. When she asked him to consider working less, he pushed back.

"I need to put in the extra time now," he said. "Once I get promoted, I'll let up."

But after his first promotion, Chase kept working just as hard. And after his second promotion. Amy pleaded with him to spend more time at home. To appease her, Chase would cut back on his hours for a while. But eventually he always resumed his long work days.

Somehow, despite the tension this created, Amy and Chase had two children, a boy named Alex and a girl named Sophia.

Amy put her career on hold to stay home with the kids. For the most part, she raised them herself. Chase was scarcely ever home.

This put a real strain on their marriage. More than once, Amy even threatened to divorce Chase if he didn't step up and do his part. Chase would apologize and promise to do better. But after a few evenings of coming home for dinner, he would always slip back into his old ways.

Chase knew he was on thin ice with Amy, but he told himself it would all be worth it when he became CEO. With each hard-won promotion, he was getting closer to that goal.

Plus, he had a feeling Amy would never really leave him. He had faith that her good grace would somehow see them through. He knew thinking that way was unfair. But at some point, it because the story he told himself.

In fact, over time, Amy learned to get by without Chase at her side. Coping with his absence was a great sadness in her life, but a sadness she chose to endure for the sake of keeping her family together.

By the time Alex and Sophia were grown and had left home, Amy had created a whole new life for herself. She'd begun working part-time for her old ad agency and teaching a marketing course at Duquesne. She also volunteered with several community organizations. Her days were full now, her distraction nearly constant.

Amy no longer expected Chase for dinner during the week. Still, she always made enough for him and set a place for him, even though she usually dined alone.

Late one afternoon, as she was making dinner, Amy heard the garage door go up. That's odd, she thought. What's Chase doing home so early?

Standing in the kitchen, she watched the door from the garage open. There stood Chase. He looked dazed.

"Chase? Are you all right?"

He stared at her blankly and said nothing. She hurried over to him.

"Chase, what's wrong? Are you okay?"

"Oh, Amy," he said, his eyes searching her face.

She waited for him to say something else, but he simply stood there, looking disoriented.

"Chase," she said, taking his hand, "let's go sit down."

She led him into the living room, and they sat next to each other on the sofa. He still said nothing. He stared at the fireplace.

She'd never seen him like this. She wondered if he was seriously ill. She thought about calling 911.

"Chase, what is it?" she said, squeezing his hands.

Finally, he turned to her and said, "I didn't get it."

"Get what?"

"Jack's job."

"What?"

"Jack called me into his office this afternoon. He told me the board decided to go with Michelle as his successor. She's younger, and they wanted a CEO who could be in place for 10 years."

"Oh, Chase. I'm so sorry."

"I gave it everything I had, Amy, but it didn't work. I've failed. I've wasted my life."

"Oh, Chase! You haven't failed or wasted your life. You've accomplished so much, and we're all so grateful."

His eyes welled with tears. She had never seen Chase cry. Now seeing him like this, she burst into tears. They clung to one another and sat there together, crying, for a long time.

One month later, after Chase's retirement had been announced and Chase and Amy had attended his big retirement party, they sat across from one another in their kitchen, eating breakfast.

"So ..." she said with a small smile.

"What?"

"What would you like to do today? You can do anything you want now, you know."

"Well, I've been thinking about that."

"And?"

"I know this might sound strange, but I think I'd like to start by spending a little time, by myself, back in the valley."

"Why?"

"I'm not sure, but I feel like I'm looking for something. I don't know what it is, but something tells me I might find it there."

"Well, then, go down in the valley. Take the time you need to find whatever you're looking for."

That's all she said. No questions. No concerns. No objections. Just grace. The grace that Chase had first found so appealing about Amy. The grace that had sustained his family all these years. Grace he did not deserve but would now be with him as he took his first steps on an uncertain new path.

Chase left for Morgantown in the morning. He got a room at SpringHill Suites in the Eastern District of the city.

Its owner, Marriott, was an Evo customer. Checking in, Chase almost mentioned that to the desk clerk but realized how utterly irrelevant that fact was to both of them. Turning my Evo brain off is going to take some time, he thought.

He got a room for just one night, not knowing how long he'd be in town. It was a hot July morning, and he decided to change into shorts and a polo shirt. Looking at himself in the wall mirror in his room, he vowed to lose some weight and get some sun on his legs.

He grabbed a cup of coffee in the hotel lobby, then drove across the river and down to Granville, where he'd grown up. He hadn't been there in years. There was no reason to go anymore. His parents had died, his brothers had moved away and he hadn't maintained any of his childhood friendships.

Chase drove slowly down his old street, Dent Avenue. Most of the houses were in disrepair. He swallowed hard as he approached his old house, a small, red-brick ranch. He glided to a stop in front of it.

The place looked so much smaller than he remembered it. Much of the grass in the front yard was brown, dried out by the mid-summer sun and, apparently, no one to water it. The trees, some of which he had helped his father plant as saplings, were now huge. The dark green Taxus bushes around the house grew wild. His father had always kept them neatly trimmed. The driveway was cracked. The old wooden front door, which his father had sanded and stained every spring, had been replaced with a red, windowless, metal door.

Chase thought about getting out and seeing if the current owner might let him take a tour. But it no longer felt like home. He decided not to intrude.

Instead, he decided to take a walk around his old neighborhood. He locked his car, hoping nobody would steal it. He got out and walked past houses he hadn't seen for decades. He still remembered every lawn he'd cut. He even remembered the neighbors who had given him tips. He remembered one older woman, Mrs. Davies, who always gave him an ice-cold Coke when he was finished in her yard. He loved cutting her grass.

Chase kept walking. He tried to find Seeger's, the corner market where he used to get groceries for his family, but it was gone. It had been converted into a house.

He walked on, across a pedestrian bridge over the Monongahela, up to WVU. He walked around the small campus, past his old classroom buildings. He was thirsty. He stopped in the student union, bought a Coke and drank it on a patio in the shade of an umbrella.

From there, he could see the river and, just beyond it, Granville. Growing up, he hadn't realized how close to the city he lived. It had seemed so distant. Morgantown seemed like a different world. It was a place which, to Chase, was both strange and alluring.

Even as a kid, he knew he would never be satisfied living in the valley. When he got to college, he realized Morgantown itself wasn't enough. So he moved to Pittsburgh and joined a company unlike anything he had ever known as a kid, where he had opportunities and experiences that would have been beyond his imagination growing up and where he eventually made more money in a year than his father had made in a lifetime.

But was it worth it? He'd sacrificed everything to become CEO of Evo, the one goal he'd set for himself 30 years earlier, but he'd fallen short.

Everyone was so polite at his retirement party, but they all knew why he was retiring. Facing those people, having to accept their congratulations with a smile, was one of the hardest things Chase had ever done. He felt like a failure.

Now what? He had far more money than he'd ever need. He was only 53. Should he go for a CEO spot somewhere else? Become a consultant? Join some corporate boards?

Such prospects left Chase cold, and they begged the question: what did he really want to do? What did he love?

As he looked down into the valley, he could almost see himself, as a boy, riding his bike to the store for his mother. He remembered how happy she looked when he'd come home with groceries, having paid for them himself. He didn't understand how much that had meant to her. All he knew is that she looked happy, and he liked making his mother happy.

Then he thought of Amy and how once he had made her happy too. But that was a long time ago. He had told himself all his hard work would one day be worth it, that then both he and Amy would be happy.

But he could see the sadness in her face, a sadness he knew he had caused, just as he now knew his longtime dream was an illusion.

Then, looking out at the river, with the sun getting low in the sky, Chase knew what he needed to do.

He needed to rededicate himself to Amy, and he needed to help people like his mother, who struggled to feed her family. He needed to share his wealth to help them get the daily essentials they could scarcely afford.

Chase felt lit up. Grace. Amy's grace. He felt wrapped in it, filled with it and saved by it.

He got up. As he did, a five dollar bill in his pocket slipped out. He'd grown used to carrying tip money. He'd forgotten the feel of it in his pocket.

Chase picked up the five, laid it on the table and set his empty Coke can on top of it. Surely somebody here could use a little extra cash.

Chase walked back down to his car on Dent Avenue and took one last look at his old house. Then he drove to his hotel, checked out and went home.

## The Secret Bookshelf

Belle Davis, the librarian at Wallace High, was getting suspicious. Over the past few days, there had been more students in the library than usual, and they seemed to be congregating in the fiction section. Most of these students left without checking out books.

Belle was busy and didn't ask questions. But after school one day, she decided to check things out.

She slowly made her way up and down the shelves of fiction books, looking for anything unusual. Everything seemed to be in order until she spotted a lower shelf with a fair number of missing books.

She knelt down and looked at the titles. *The Adventures of Huckleberry Finn, Catcher in the Rye, To Kill a Mockingbird, The Handmaid's Tale, Of Mice and Men, Leaves of Grass, Diary of a Young Girl* ... all familiar titles. There were other books on the shelf too, with titles Belle didn't recognize.

But wait. Something's off, she thought. *Leaves of Grass* is poetry, and *Diary of a Young Girl* is non-fiction. What are they doing here?

Then she realized what all these books had in common. They'd been banned or challenged. They shouldn't be here or in any public library in Texas, she thought.

Belle skimmed the titles on all the other shelves in that section. They were all fiction books whose titles weren't in question.

Belle was about to remove the banned books but stopped. She knew she needed to report this to Bonnie Jackson, the school's young principal, and that Bonnie should see all the books on this shelf just as Belle had found them.

So she turned off the lights, locked up and went downstairs to see Bonnie. But she'd left for the day, so Belle decided she'd stop by her office first thing in the morning.

The following morning, Belle showed Bonnie the suspect bookshelf in the library.

"How long have these books been here?" Bonnie said with a look of concern.

"I don't know."

"Who put them here?"

"I'm not sure," Belle said, detecting an accusatory tone in Bonnie's voice. "It wasn't me."

"Well, we need to find out. Take some photos of all these books, then put them in a box. Bring the box to my office."

"Okay," Bonnie said.

The school quietly launched an investigation. What administrators learned from talking to students is that one of the school's teachers was responsible for creating this special bookshelf in the library and keeping it stocked with banned or challenged books.

However, none of the students would disclose the teacher's name. So Bonnie called together all the school's teachers during lunch break. She explained the situation and asked whomever was responsible to come forward either then or after the meeting.

Most of the teachers looked around, shaking their heads. Some looked anxious, others angry. A low murmur rippled throughout the conference room.

Then a teacher standing in the back said, "I'm responsible."

Everyone looked in her direction. It was Hayley Monroe, a 50-something woman who taught English. She was one of the school's most popular and longest-serving teachers. Except for a few gasps, the room was silent.

"Hayley?" someone whispered.

Hayley simply stood there, looking at Bonnie, and said nothing. Bonnie looked surprised. She wasn't expecting anyone to confess, at least not in that public setting.

Nor had she suspected Hayley of doing something like this. She'd been a model teacher at the school for more than 25 years, with not so much as one complaint against her. Bonnie had lost track of how many times Hayley had been named teacher of the year.

Bonnie realized the seriousness of the situation, especially with book bans being such an emotional and politically charged issue in Texas and many other places at the moment. Something like this could give Wallace High a black eye. She knew she'd have to handle this case with care.

Chatter in the room began to grow louder.

"Okay, everyone," Bonnie said. "This meeting is over. I'll talk with Hayley, and I'm sure we'll resolve this matter soon. Until we do, I would ask that you all keep this confidential, out of respect for Hayley and the school."

Everyone but Hayley and Bonnie filed out. A few of the teachers patted Hayley on the back or gave her hugs as they left.

Finally, when everyone else was gone, Bonnie said, "Let's have a seat."

They sat down across from each other at the conference table. Bonnie's hands were folded on the table.

"Why don't you begin?" she said.

"What would you like to know?"

"Well, for starters, why did you do it?"

"I think it's important that our students have access to these books."

"So why didn't you ask if you could make them available?"

"Because I knew what the answer would be."

"And so you just went ahead and did this?"

"Yes."

"Was anyone else involved?"

"No. Only me."

Bonnie looked serious.

"Hayley, what you've done is illegal in the state of Texas. It's also a violation of our district's policy. You know that. We went over it at the beginning of the year."

"Yes, I know."

Now Bonnie looked agitated.

"Well, you've left me no option but to take disciplinary action," she said.

Hayley looked at Bonnie like a teacher might look at a student in need, with understanding eyes. In fact, 20 years earlier, Bonnie had been a student in Hayley's English class. Hayley had been one of Bonnie's favorite teachers at Wallace High. This made the current situation all the harder for Bonnie.

"Bonnie, I've known you a long time, and I've only ever known you to be thoughtful and fair. I know you have to do your job, and I trust you'll be fair."

By the time Bonnie got back to her office, a reporter from the local newspaper was calling. He had the whole story, including Hayley's name. He didn't disclose his source, but clearly one of the teachers had leaked it. He asked Bonnie if the school had a statement and if Hayley would be fired.

"I can only tell you we're going to do a full and fair investigation," Bonnie said.

"But if it's true, won't you need to let this teacher go?"

"I'm not going to speculate on the outcome of our investigation," Bonnie said before hanging up.

But the word was out. Within the hour, she began getting calls from parents. That afternoon, the local paper ran a story online. It immediately got picked up more broadly. By the end of the day, the now not-so-secret bookshelf at Wallace High was national news and all over social media.

The following day, Bonnie met with the president of the local school board, Abby Rogers, and the district's attorney, Trey Parker. After listening to Bonnie, Rogers told her to launch a formal investigation. Parker instructed her how to go about it.

"What then?" Bonnie said.

Rogers and Parker looked at each other.

"You'll make a decision," Rogers said, "and that should be the end of it."

"I don't think you understand," Bonnie said. "Hayley Monroe is an extremely popular teacher at our school. Our students are already taking her side in this. Even a few parents have spoken out to support her. If I let Hayley go, I assure you that will not be the end of it."

Even as Bonnie launched a formal investigation, students at the high school began holding daily rallies in support of Hayley. These events attracted more media attention, and the case became a big news story, with both supporters and critics of Hayley speaking out locally and nationally.

The main issue was not so much the specific books that had been found on the secret shelf in the school's library. It was that such a bookshelf had been set up and maintained on school property as well as the state's definition of "unsuitable" books for high schoolers.

Few took exception to classics like *Catcher in the Rye* being available in public schools. But many parents were angry that books about queer teens were also on that shelf. Some were upset that books which featured racial epithets were there too, even if they were written by venerable authors like Twain and Steinbeck.

And of course, local politicians, sensing voter discontent, also weighed in.

"Ultimately, this is an issue of abiding by the law and allowing parents to determine what their children will be subjected to in our schools," said one state senator.

Almost overnight, the secret bookshelf had become a new flashpoint in a philosophical debate over free speech and parental control.

Bonnie was getting pressure from the school board to act. After school one day, she called Hayley to her office.

"I'm very sorry to have to do this, Hayley," she said, unable to look her in the eye. "But I'm afraid I have no choice but to dismiss you as a teacher here."

Hayley, of course, saw it coming. Still, she felt like crying.

"I understand," she said, maintaining her composure. "I have only one request."

"What's that?"

"Would you let me speak before the school board?"

Hayley thought for a moment.

"I think that's fair," she said. "You deserve to be heard."

"Thank you."

The next local board of education meeting was held in the main county courtroom to accommodate the large crowd expected. Every seat was taken. Rogers sat elevated in the judge's chair, flanked by the other board members. Reporters, some with TV cameras, lined the back of the room.

Hayley was scheduled to speak at the end of the meeting, the only item under "new business." Of course, she was the reason everyone was there.

When Hayley's time came, Rogers briefly summarized the situation. She explained the school's decision to fire Hayley "in accord with this district's policy and state law." She then invited her to speak.

Hayley walked up to the lectern at the front of the center aisle. She carried a single note card. When she got to the lectern, she leaned into the microphone and said, "Thank you."

Then she put on her reading glasses and read from the card.

"'It's difficult in times like these: ideals, dreams and cherished hopes rise within us, only to be crushed by grim reality. It's a wonder I haven't abandoned all my ideals, they seem so absurd and impractical. Yet I cling to them because I still believe, in spite of everything, that people are truly good at heart.'"

Hayley took off her glasses and looked up at Bonnie and the other board members.

"These are the words of Anne Frank," she said, "words she wrote as she and her family hid from the Nazis, words in a famous book our children may not read because, here in Texas, the state has decided *Diary of a Young Girl* is unsuitable for them. I do not question the responsibility of our government to protect us. But I do question whether it's right for our government to decide, arbitrarily, what is and is not suitable for our children to read. My decision to make banned books available to students at Wallace High School in the school library may not have been wise. But I don't regret making those books available to my students. I know these young people. They're good and thoughtful people, and I trust them. I trust them to read novels like *The Adventures of Huckleberry Finn* and form their own thoughts and opinions about racism and decide which words they will and will not use in their lives. Losing my job, a job that I've loved in a school that I've loved for more than 25 years, is hard. But at least I know I've given my students every opportunity to learn for themselves, to read books which some might find unsuitable but most of the world considers literature of the highest order. I suspect many of us in this room grew up reading at least some of these books. I'll never forget reading *To Kill a Mockingbird* for the first time. It changed my life. It expanded me. What a shame that young people in this state can no longer find such a magnificent book in our libraries."

She paused.

"I've come here tonight not to contest my firing but to ask this school board to define what is and isn't suitable for our children to read. I urge you not to rely on the state to make this determination. The state will never define unsuitable because to do that would mean being specific about what it is about any given book that our children must not see. The state wants to keep 'unsuitable' vague because then it can decide which books will be banned and no one in this room or anywhere else in the state of Texas can disagree."

She paused again and cleared her throat.

"Teaching at Wallace High School has been the greatest honor of my life. I will miss it dearly, but I will move on, and you will still be left to answer a simple but very important question. Will you allow the state to decide what's suitable for our children to read or will you have a voice in that?"

With that, Hayley turned around and walked back to her seat. As she did, the courtroom was silent. Then someone began clapping. Then many joined in. Then most people rose and applauded for several minutes.

Seated, Hayley looked around with a small smile, her only way to fight back the tears.

Finally, everyone sat down, and Abby Rogers said, "Thank you, Ms. Monroe. The board appreciates your comments and will consider your suggestion. This session has now concluded. Thank you all for coming."

Reporters and TV crews surrounded Hayley in the atrium outside the courtroom, but she waved them off.

"I have nothing to add to my comments to the board," she said, walking away.

The following week, the school board did briefly discuss Hayley's suggestion to define unsuitable for books in public school libraries in the district but opted to continue to be guided by the state.

"Every school district in Texas follows the state's policy," one board member said. "Why should we be the outlier?"

In the meantime, students at Wallace started holding protests after school nearly every day. Then they began protesting outside the city's public library. These protests continued to attract news coverage, most of it critical of Wallace and the school board.

That summer, Hayley had a booth at the city's annual book festival. There she sold copies of books that had been banned and challenged by the state, with the proceeds going to a campaign urging the state to be clear about why it bans books.

Her booth had attracted media coverage. That year, it was the most popular booth at the festival. Many people brought their own copies of banned books for Hayley to sell. Many told Hayley how sorry they were that she was fired.

Public opinion in Texas was changing. A growing number of people now opposed efforts to have books removed from their local libraries, and most were now in favor of the state disclosing why it had decided to ban certain books.

As public opinion changed, politicians started speaking out against bans and for more disclosure. Eventually, the state was forced to clarify why, title by title, it was banning books and stop using "unsuitable" as a reason.

Now there was public discussion at the local level about whether certain books should be banned. As a result, some books continued to be banned, but the majority of previously banned titles returned to public libraries.

And it would never have happened without Hayley Monroe and her secret bookshelf.

## Time to Choose

I ran into Chicago Union Station about 10 minutes before my train was set to depart for St. Louis. I'd overslept. Two months into retirement, I still hadn't gotten into a new sleep rhythm.

I was one of the last passengers to board, so it wasn't hard to spot my open seat, a window seat in coach. An old man was in the aisle seat. He was wearing a denim shirt and wire-rimmed glasses and had a scruffy beard and a ponytail. He looked like an ancient hippie.

I stuffed my bag in the overhead above him, but he didn't get up.

"Excuse me," I said.

He looked up, as if he was just realizing I was there.

"Oh, I'm sorry," he said, slowly stepping into the aisle.

I squeezed by, laptop in hand, and sat down. The old man then sat back down. He folded his hands on his lap. He didn't have a device or a book, and he didn't say a word. I figured he was one of those guys who didn't like to talk on trains. After sitting next to more than my fair share of windbags on flights over the years, I respected that.

As we pulled out of the station, though, he said, "Where you heading?"

"St. Louis. You?"

"West Coast."

I nodded. I thought he might say something else, but he pushed his seat back, closed his eyes and fell asleep.

I pulled down the tray table and opened my laptop.

About 15 minutes later, the old man woke up and looked around, as if he were getting his bearings. He looked at me, then past me, out the window.

"Beautiful day," I said.

He looked at me and smiled.

"Yes," he said.

I felt my watch vibrate. I tapped the face. It was a text from Catherine. She was already on a break on the first day of her conference in Washington. She wanted to let me know it was off to a good start and wish me safe travel.

I tapped my watch twice, held it held close to my mouth and said, "Good. Period. Train left on time. Period. Let you know when I get there. Period." Then I tapped it again.

I looked up. The old man was looking at me.

"My wife," I said.

"Oh."

He stared at my watch, as if he were trying to figure it out.

"So where on the West Coast are you heading?" I said.

"LA."

"Great city."

"Never been there."

"What brings you there?"

"The weather."

After a long pause, he said, "I just couldn't face another winter in Maine."

"Sometimes I feel that way about Chicago."

"What brings you to St. Louis?"

"I'm just going to hang out there for a couple of days while my wife's away. Probably go up in the Arch. Take in a Cardinals game."

"Sounds fun."

"Hope so. I've been to St. Louis many times on business, but never for pleasure. I'm looking forward to it."

"What business are you in, if you don't mind me asking."

"Not at all. I've actually just retired. I was in advertising for 40 years."

"Congratulations."

"Thanks. It still feels strange to say I'm retired."

"I'll bet."

"What about you? Still working?"

I assumed this guy was retired too but wanted to be charitable.

"I just quit my job a few days ago," he said.

"Really? What kind of work to you do, if you don't mind me asking."

"Dish washer."

"Pardon me?"

"I wash dishes. I've washed dishes for over 50 years."

I wasn't sure what to say.

"It's okay," he said with a small smile. "It's not as glamorous as advertising, but it's a living."

"Absolutely."

I wasn't sure what else to say.

Finally, I said, "Have you been to St. Louis?"

"No."

I nodded.

About a minute later, he said, "I've only been out of Maine once."

"Really?"

"Yeah."

"Where did you go?"

"Vietnam."

Holy crap, I thought.

"Were you in the Army?"

"Yeah."

"When did you serve?"

"In the late sixties."

I was too young to have served in Vietnam, but I knew the late sixties were the deadliest years of the war.

"Did you see action?"

"Yes."

"Were you wounded?"

"Not physically."

Now I really didn't know what to say.

"But I saw a lot of people who were wounded or killed."

"I'm sorry."

"Me too."

Once again, I was at a loss for words.

Then, after an awkward silence, he said, "When I came back, I had a hard time adjusting. All I wanted to do was stay home."

I nodded.

"But I had a wife and a young daughter to support. So I got the first job I could find: washing dishes at a local restaurant. I never imagined I'd be washing dishes all these years. Growing up, I wanted to be a doctor. But what I saw, and did, in Vietnam changed me. It broke me. I was never the same."

"I understand. At least you were able to provide for your family."

"Yeah, for a while. But I was a lousy husband and father. Eventually, my wife left me, and she took our daughter with her. I haven't seen either of them for 50 years."

"I'm sorry."

"Thanks. Anyway, I just kept washing dishes, and I never left Maine. I've pretty much kept to myself all these years."

"What will you do when you get to LA?"

"I don't know. Look for a place to live, I guess. I've saved a bit, and my sister's going to mail me my Social Security and disability checks. So I guess I'll be okay. I don't need much. Just a place in the sun, a place where I can finally feel whole again."

"I'm sorry your life has been so hard," I said. "I hope this will be a good move for you."

"Me too."

I looked at my watch. We still had four hours to go to get to St. Louis. I sensed this guy was kind of talked out, so I re-opened my laptop. I skimmed the news headlines. The top stories were about the war in Afghanistan. I felt lucky to have been too young to fight in Vietnam and that my son never had to go to war.

I thought about my family. My career had demanded a lot of me. I was absent from the lives of my wife and children far too much. I had shortchanged my loved ones. That was my greatest regret.

I hardly saw my kids anymore, and I knew I'd never have much time with them again. That made me sad. But I figured that, when I retired, Catherine and I would finally have time together.

But I discovered that, over the years, she had created a whole new life for herself. She'd become a life coach. When I was working, I wasn't really aware of how much time she was devoting to this. I had no idea she'd become such an expert or how well regarded she was in the field. She'd never talked much about her work. Or if she had, I wasn't listening.

We'd once been so close. But we had drifted apart. At some point, our lives began spinning in different orbits.

Now Catherine was now a speaker in demand. That weekend, she was speaking at a conference in Washington.

I thought retirement would be different. I deliberately hadn't planned to do anything right away. I thought I'd give myself some time to decompress and consider my options. But so far, I felt adrift and alone.

I looked over at the old man. He was sleeping. I thought about his lonely life. I thought about his decision to finally quit washing dishes, the only thing he'd ever done, and leave Maine, the only place he'd ever lived. I admired his courage.

He woke up when lunch was served, and we chatted over turkey wraps and coffee. When we got to St. Louis, I finally introduced myself.

"By the way, I'm Tom," I said, extending my hand.

"I'm Alan," he said, taking it.

At that point, last names seemed too formal.

"I hope you enjoy LA," I said. "And thank you for your service."

"Thanks. And you're welcome."

I took an Uber to my hotel and checked in. My room overlooked Busch Stadium. I'd planned to go to the game that evening.

But then I thought about the prospect of sitting in the ballpark and watching the game by myself and coming back to this room and sleeping alone. I thought about Alan. He no longer had a wife. I did. But once again, even without a job to call me away, I'd left her to do my own thing.

Is this what my retirement is going to be like, I thought, just an extension of the ego trip that had been my career? Am I, like Alan, destined to be on my own?

I thought about Catherine. She was probably speaking to a big audience at that very moment. And then, probably after dinner with people who appreciated her, she too would go back to a hotel room and sleep alone.

I thought about Alan. He was probably in Kansas by now. He was choosing to make a new life for himself. He was on his way to find a place where he might finally feel whole again. I longed to find such a place.

I opened my laptop, went online and bought an airline ticket to Washington for that evening. It will be tight, I thought, but I can make it.

## The Architect

David Finnegan pulled a pair of socks from his dresser and sat down to put them on. He was about to slip a sock over his right foot when he noticed an "L" on the toe.

Damn, he thought. Even my socks tell me what to do.

Frustrated but resigned, he put his socks on correctly and finished getting dressed for work.

"You're late," his wife Laura said as he came downstairs.

"Good morning," he said, stepping toward the kitchen.

"Where are you going?"

"I need coffee."

"No time. You can get some at work."

He stopped, hoping she might cut him some slack.

"Henry's waiting," she said, opening the front door. "Remember we've got dinner at six. You'll need to leave the office by five."

"I'll remember," he said.

He stopped to give her a kiss. But as he came close, she turned her head, so he kissed her on the cheek.

"Have a good day," he said.

"You too," she said, closing the door behind him.

"Morning, Henry," David said to his driver as he opened the rear door of the black Mercedes-Benz.

"Good morning, Mr. Finnegan," Henry said. "Beautiful day."

"Yes, it is," David said, getting in.

He laid his briefcase on the seat and pulled out his cell phone. It was a 30-minute drive to his office. Thirty minutes to see what lay in store for him that day.

He scanned his calendar. Back-to-back meetings, every one designed to get him to say yes to something.

David had worked hard for nearly 30 years to become CEO of Savio Industries. The whole time he had imagined what it would be like to be in charge of a large company, to be able to tell people what to do.

But the reality of being CEO was not like that at all. From the moment he took over, David had been told what to do, what to think and what to say. He was surrounded by handlers. He was no longer his own man.

Driving home from dinner that evening, David said to Laura, "I'm thinking of taking some time off."

"Why?"

"I need a break."

"We'll be taking a vacation in June."

"I know, but I don't need another vacation."

"What do you need then?"

"I think I need to go away."

"And do what?"

"I don't know."

"David, you're the CEO of Savio. You can't just go away."

"Why not?"

"You're serious."

"Laura, I might be the CEO of Savio, but most days I feel like the least powerful person in the company."

She laughed.

"But you're the CEO! You're the *most* powerful person in the company."

"Then why is it that every time I try to advance an idea of my own about 10 people try to talk me out of it?"

"Maybe you need to push back."

My wife thinks I'm a wimp, he thought.

"Laura, I haven't had a day off in years. I'm tired. I just need a break."

"Maybe you could go fishing," she said sarcastically.

"Thanks for listening," he said, pulling into their driveway.

On his way into his office the following morning, he called his secretary, Katie, who was always in early.

"Please clear my calendar today," he said.

"Pardon me?"

"And tell Megan I'd like to see her in my office at ten."

"Okay," Katie said, sounding tentative. "Should I tell her the purpose?"

"No."

"Okay."

When David arrived, Katie gave him a curious look and said, "Is everything all right?"

"Yes. Were you able to cancel my meetings today?"

"I'm in the process of doing that."

"Good. Were you able to schedule Megan?"

"Yes. She'll be here at ten."

"Good."

"Is there anything else?"

"Yes. Two things. First, please ask Damon to come up at eleven. Second, please drop the distribution list for the board into a draft email for me. I'm going to send them a note."

Katie gave him another curious look. David only wanted to see Damon, his Communications VP, when there was big news or the company was in trouble, and Katie always handled his correspondence with board members.

But before she could say anything, David thanked her, went into his office and closed his door.

He hung up his suit coat and sat down at his desk. He opened his top drawer, pulled out a legal pad and plucked a pen from a coffee mug on his desk.

He drafted this note:

Dear Fellow Savio Board Members,

After deep reflection, I have decided to take a one-month sabbatical, beginning next Monday.

I am putting Megan Shepard in charge in my absence. Megan is very familiar with all our plans and eminently qualified to fill in for me.

In case you're wondering, my health is fine, and there are no emergencies at home. I simply need this time to recharge. I expect to return in a month, ready to resume my duties as CEO.

We will announce this move through a news release at 3:00 p.m. ET today.

Thanks for your understanding and your support for Megan while I'm away.

David Finnegan

He looked over his note and made a few, small edits. Then he opened his laptop, typed his note into the folder Katie had created and pushed "draft."

David closed his laptop, turned around in his chair and looked out his enormous window. He was going to think through what he wanted to say to Megan, but the Empire State Building caught his eye.

He'd seen the Art Deco skyscraper so many times over the years that it simply blended into the Midtown Manhattan skyline. Now, though, the magnificent structure glistened in the morning sunlight, and he remembered reading the facade is made up of limestone panels sourced from a quarry in Indiana, close to where he'd grown up.

He remembered learning that in grade school, when he first dreamed of becoming an architect, years before his father had insisted David major in business in college.

The following morning, David and Laura were having breakfast in their kitchen.

"You're really going to go through with this," Laura said.

"It's just a month. If you need me, you can call me anytime."

She shook her head.

"David, this is so unlike you. Are you sure you're okay?"

"I'm fine. I just need a break. Maybe it'll be a nice break for you too."

"What does that mean?"

"I don't know. Sometimes I feel like a nuisance around here."

"Hey, this is *your* break, not mine."

"You're right. I'm sorry."

"So are you just going to drive around for a month?"

"No. I thought I'd drive to Bloomington for starters. I'm not sure where I'll go from there."

"Is that what this is about? Going home?"

"No. *This* is my home. I just haven't been to Bloomington in a long time."

She shook her head again.

"Look," he said, "I know this all might sound crazy to you, but I haven't done anything for myself in years. Sometimes I feel like I'm the only one *not* in charge of my life. So for one month, I'm going to steer my own course for a change. After 30 years, I think I deserve a little break."

"Well, I hope you have fun."

He had hoped she might be more supportive. Now he realized he should have known better. When it came to their home life, Laura had called the shots for years. He hadn't consulted her on this, and she was pissed.

David didn't like upsetting his wife. But he hadn't been his own man for a long time, and he felt that, if he didn't get away now, he might never find himself again.

The following morning, Laura trailed David to the front door. He gave her a hug and went in for a kiss, but she turned her head, and he again kissed her cheek. She's still pissed, he thought.

"I'll be in touch," he said.

"Safe travel."

Then she turned and walked away.

David knew the way to Bloomington, even though he hadn't made the 12-hour drive for years. He'd begun flying there 20 years earlier. He'd gone back to see his parents every year.

Now he hadn't been there for three years. He'd flown in to be with his mother when she was very ill and, soon after, for her funeral.

He knew Pittsburgh was about halfway. He figured he'd stop there for the night but didn't book a hotel. When he traveled, Katie handled all his arrangements. Now he was on his own. The very idea brought a smile to his face.

When their kids were little, David and Laura had stopped in Pittsburgh on their way to Bloomington. That's the last time he'd been there. He couldn't remember where they stayed, only that they'd ridden an incline up to an old neighborhood called Mount Washington, where they had dinner and looked out over the city.

At a rest stop, David booked a room at the Sheraton in downtown Pittsburgh. He got there mid-afternoon, checked in and took the Monongahela Incline up to Mount Washington.

He looked down on the city from Grandview Overlook. It was a clear day, and the blue waters of the three rivers far below shimmered in the late afternoon sun. He remembered being there with his family and pointing out how the Allegheny and Monongahela come together to form the Ohio.

His kids were excited and scrambled for the coin-operated binoculars to get a closer look, and Laura seemed impressed. Those were the days when he still impressed her.

He had a vague recollection of the Mount Washington neighborhood. He mainly remembered it was old. Now he had nowhere to be and decided to check it out.

He strolled down Shiloh Street, lined with shops and restaurants, gazed at the city from a bench in Emerald View Park and followed narrow, cobblestone streets through dozens of old houses. He knew from his architecture classes in college that some of these houses had been built in the late 1800s and the more modern ones in the 1930s.

All of them seemed to be in pretty good shape. David imagined all the frigid, windswept winters they had endured. He marveled that they'd stood the test of time.

The sun was beginning to set, and he was hungry. He ducked into a tavern called Shiloh Gastro, whose menu boasted the "best mac and cheese and pierogis in town." He tried both and felt a little guilty, knowing Laura would frown on such comfort foods.

In the morning, over breakfast at the hotel, David booked a room for that night at the Holiday Inn in Bloomington. Then he headed west on I-70.

In Ohio, the terrain began to flatten out and look a lot more like Indiana, with vast fields of corn, wheat and soybeans. David rolled down his window and took in the earthy smells, which reminded him of his childhood. He stopped in Indianapolis for lunch, then headed south to Bloomington.

He checked into his hotel, changed clothes and drove to the neighborhood where he'd grown up. He parked across the street from his old house, a small, three-bedroom ranch with light yellow brick. His parents had built it in the 1960s and lived there nearly 60 years.

It was now painted white, and the trees in the yard were huge. The place looked old. David was tempted to get out and look around and maybe take a tour, if the owners were home. But he suspected the place had been remodeled, and he preferred to think of it as it was when he was a kid.

He drove on to Rose Hill Cemetery, where his parents were buried. He found their small, flat headstones, knelt in the grass and said a silent prayer.

David's mother had always been his biggest champion. In her eyes, he could do no wrong. His father, who had never made much money, wanted his son to do well financially. When David announced he wanted to study architecture in college, his father insisted he major in business.

"If you want to take some classes in architecture, fine, but you're going to get a degree in business," his father said firmly.

Given his father was paying his tuition, David didn't have room to argue, though he did manage to make architecture into a minor at the University of Indiana.

That was no small feat. IU's architecture school was located in Columbus, Indiana, an hour east of the main campus in Bloomington. David didn't have a car, so he had to take a bus there, but he didn't mind the commute. He loved learning about architecture. He majored in finance for his father but minored in architecture for himself.

Now he decided to drive to Columbus to see the Eskenazi School of Art, Architecture and Design. It was now a sprawling collection of 65 academic buildings, art galleries and studios throughout the city. He wished the school had been so innovative and expansive when he was a student.

Touring the low-slung, modernist Republic Building, the centerpiece of the Eskenazi School, David was reminded of Frank Lloyd Wright's original house and studio in Oak Park, Illinois. His class had taken a field trip there his junior year. David had been enthralled. Now he felt called to go back and see it again.

He drove back to Bloomington. That evening, over a cheeseburger, fries and a beer at the bar in his hotel, he booked a room at the Carleton Hotel in Oak Park for the following night and bought a ticket online to tour Frank Lloyd Wright's place.

He texted Laura to keep her posted. He missed her. At the same time, he knew that, if she were with him, she would be bored — and no doubt be giving him hell for his poor food choices.

In the morning, he took off for Oak Park, four hours north. Making his way through tough Chicago traffic, he checked into his hotel, grabbed lunch and headed for Frank Lloyd Wright's place.

Touring it, David remembered not only being in awe of the design when he was in college, but toying with the idea of switching his major to architecture. He knew that would mean his father would no longer pay his tuition. But maybe he could make enough money that summer to cover the cost of his final year at IU.

By the time he got back to Bloomington after that field trip, though, David had resigned himself to getting a business degree. Not because he couldn't have paid his own way his senior year. But because he knew not getting a degree in business would have broken his father's heart.

Now, as he marveled at the clean, smooth lines of Wright's original home, he wondered how different his life would have been if he had followed his dream, formed in grade school when he learned about those limestone panels quarried for the Empire State Building just a few miles from his original home in Bloomington.

But he hadn't followed that dream. Instead, he'd chosen to make his father happy, then Laura, then his bosses, then his shareholders, board members and handlers. He'd made them all happy not by building anything but by maintaining everything.

David was expected to grow Savio's business by two or three percent a year, and he knew how to do that. Launch a new product line. Pick up a few new customers. Expand into a new market. Safe plays.

Now David stood in a house whose designer had not played it safe, and he felt inspired to be bold like Frank Lloyd Wright.

He picked up a brochure featuring 16 of his houses open for tours. He circled six he thought he could visit during the balance of his sabbatical — in Illinois, Indiana, Pennsylvania and New York.

The very idea lit him up. When he got back to his hotel, David texted Laura to tell her about his plan.

"Interesting," she replied.

He wasn't sure if she was being facetious or sincere. There was a time when she did think of him as interesting. He hoped she might think of him that way again.

Regardless, David was tired of worrying about what others thought he should do. It was time for him to be his own man. It was time for him to build.

David got home with two days to spare on his sabbatical. Laura greeted him in the foyer with a warm hug and a kiss on the lips.

"I missed you," she said.

"I missed you too."

"Leave your stuff here," she said, taking his hand. "I want to hear all about your trip."

They went into the family room and sat on the sofa. She turned toward him and tucked her feet under her, like she used to many years earlier.

David had kept her posted on each of the Frank Lloyd Wright houses he had visited and sent her photos. At first, he wasn't sure how much detail to share, but she seemed genuinely interested, so he told her all about each of the houses and how seeing all of them had inspired him to think differently about Savio Industries and his role as CEO.

"I've been a steward," he said. "Now I feel called to be an architect."

"Tell me about that," Laura said with a smile.

He told her he wanted to divest Savio's auto repair, aviation maintenance and property management businesses and acquire design firms and building supply businesses.

"Savio is going to become a builder," he said. "We're going to create."

Laura looked at him the way she used to when they were just starting out. It had been a long time, but David still knew that look.

## Conversation on a Park Bench

I spotted him sitting on a bench in a park whose wood-chip trail I'd begun walking on weekends, now that it was spring and our long, hard winter was over.

He was an old man. His hair was white and shaggy. He wore horn-rimmed glasses. He was well dressed, with a dark blue sport coat and a yellow tie, but his clothes were rumpled. His hands rested on a cane whose tip was buried in wood chips. He was looking my way.

"Good morning," I said as I approached him.

"Good morning."

I couldn't help but stare. He looked just like one of my favorite authors, Ray Bradbury. Of course, it could not be him. Bradbury had been gone for years.

I stopped a few feet short of the bench. He was looking up at me and smiling.

"Have we met?" I said.

"In a way, yes."

I wasn't sure what he meant by that.

"You look so familiar," I said.

"I get that a lot."

"Has anyone ever told you that you look like ..."

"Ray Bradbury?"

"Yeah."

"All the time," he said with chuckle. "Would you like to sit down?"

"Sure. I'm Jason," I said, extending my hand.

"Hi, Jason," he said, taking it. "I'm Ray."

"Ray?"

"Yes."

"As in Ray Bradbury?"

"Well, yes. That's the name my parents gave me."

"But you're ..."

"Dead?"

"Yeah!"

"So I'm told."

"I don't understand."

"Well, it is confusing, I suppose. After all, I did die — in California, in 2012."

"But then how can you be ..."

"Here?"

"Yeah."

"My writing keeps me alive. It keeps me alive for anyone whom my words have touched. I know that includes you, Jason."

For a moment, I thought maybe this guy was a nut, someone who impersonated Ray Bradbury. But who in the world would do that? Besides, he looked *exactly* like Bradbury. I'd seen pictures of him and watched a documentary about him. He even *sounds* like Bradbury, I thought. I decided to go along.

"With respect," I said, "how do you know your words have touched me?"

"When I write — when I wrote, that is — it's as if I'm looking in a mirror, and in that mirror, I can see myself and my reader. In my story, we are together. I first saw you long ago, when you were a teenager."

"*Fahrenheit 451.*"

"Yes. You were in Mrs. Turnbull's class."

Good lord, I thought. He really does know me.

"It was the first book I ever read," I said. "I mean the first *real* book."

He smiled.

"I'm honored," he said.

"Do you remember the first book you read?"

"I sure do. *The War of the Worlds* by H.G. Wells. I read it as a boy."

"How was it?"

"How was it? I fell in love! By the time I finished that book, I knew I wanted to be a writer."

"You found your calling."

"Yes."

"Ever look back?"

"Not once."

"Well, you were a great writer."

"Thank you."

A woman strolled by us.

"Good morning," she said.

"Good morning," Ray said.

Once she'd passed, I said, "Do you know her?"

"In a way. She read *The Martian Chronicles* in high school."

I laughed.

"You knew a lot of people," I said.

"It was the greatest blessing of my life."

I shook my head.

"What?" he said.

"It's just ... it's hard to believe you're actually here."

"Kind of fitting, don't you think, given the kind of stuff I wrote?"

"Do you mean science fiction?"

"Actually, I didn't write much science fiction."

"You didn't?"

"No. Science fiction is a depiction of the real. Fantasy is a depiction of the unreal. I wrote fantasy."

"I see. So why did you do it?"

"What? Write?"

"Yeah."

"If I hadn't written every day, the poisons would have accumulated, and I would have begun to die or act crazy or both."

"You wrote every day?"

"From the time I first picked up a pen, I wrote every day of my life. And near the end, when I could no longer hold a pen, I dictated to my daughter from my bed."

"That's amazing."

"It was a great life. I did what I loved."

"Cool."

We were both silent for a moment.

"So have you kept up with things, you know, down here?"

"Not really. What have I missed?"

"Let's see. Well, we're not burning books, like Montag did, but we're banning them."

"Why?"

"To protect children."

"From what?"

"Violence. Racism. Offensive language. You name it."

"Which books?"

"*Animal Farm*, *Huckleberry Finn* and, I'm sorry to tell you, *Fahrenheit 451,* among many others. I heard the other day *Charlotte's Web* has been banned."

He winced.

"You know, you don't have to burn books to destroy a culture," he said. "You just have to get people to stop reading them."

"Good point."

"What else have I missed?"

"Artificial Intelligence, I guess. It's called AI."

"What is it?"

"It's the simulation of human intelligence by computers."

"Do you mean like IBM's Watson?"

"Well, yes, but much more advanced."

"Talk about science fiction. How does it work?"

"AI analyzes large amounts of data for patterns and uses those patterns to make predictions about the future. One chatbot, for example ..."

"Hang on. Chatbot?"

"Sorry. A chatbot is a computer program that simulates human conversation, either written or spoken, and allows people to interact with digital devices as if they were communicating with a real person. One popular chatbot, called ChatGPT, can even create realistic text."

"Like short stories?"

"More like research papers. But yeah, short stories too. Even novels."

"Are they any good?"

"Well, the technology is still being improved, but a lot of the stuff ChatGPT is generating is pretty good."

"Well, I still love books," he said. "Nothing a computer can do will ever compare to a book. You can't really put a book on the Internet. All the computer can give you is a manuscript. People don't want to read manuscripts. They want to read books, books written by human beings."

"I think most people would agree with you."

"Besides, where's the beauty in something written by a computer? 'It was a pleasure to burn.' That's the opening line in *Fahrenheit 451*. I defy a computer to come up with something that beautiful."

I smiled. I'd heard Bradbury had a healthy ego.

"That *is* a pretty good line," I said.

"It's a damned good line!"

"Yes, it is."

He nodded.

"What else is new?" he said.

"Well, I guess since you've been gone, our society has become very divided. We can't seem to agree on much of anything anymore. And we're always fighting."

"I saw that once, in the 1960s."

"I wasn't around then, but I think it's different now. In the 1960s, people protested. We still have protests, but we hardly talk to each other anymore. We fight on social media."

"Social media?"

"You know, like Twitter."

"Oh, yeah."

"Some people are online all the time."

"Well, at least they're communicating."

"That's just it. They're not *really* communicating. They're being fed content that supports their interests and points of view. And they're doing all that on laptops and phones, not face to face. A lot of people, especially younger people, don't have many meaningful relationships these days. People are lonely, especially after Covid."

"Covid?"

"I'll tell you about that some other time."

"Books," he said.

"Books?"

"Yes, books. Books bring people together."

"I agree. Unfortunately, most people aren't reading books anymore. They read text messages and emails and news headlines, but not books."

"Well, there's your problem."

"How so?"

His face was red. I hoped I hadn't upset him.

"Don't you see?" he said, raising his voice and stamping his cane. "You've got to stuff your eyes with wonder, live as if you'd drop dead in 10 seconds. See the world. It's more fantastic than any dream made in factories or, as you might say, generated by ChatGPT."

As I listened, I realized this man had lived in a world where people were much more connected.

"Most people today are hunkered down," I said. "They're afraid of the world. They don't want to stuff their eyes with wonder anymore. They've seen enough, and all they want is to be left alone."

"It sounds like people are stuck in their heads."

"Yeah, maybe that's it."

"Well, then, maybe *that's* the real problem. If we listened to our intellect we'd never have a love affair. We'd never have a friendship. We'd never go into business because we'd be cynical. But that's ridiculous. If you listen to your intellect, you're going to miss life. You've got to jump off cliffs all the time and build your wings on the way down."

"Is that how you approached your work?"

"Honestly, I didn't think about it that much," he said. "I just wrote. I loved writing, and I had to do what I loved. And I wanted to leave something behind. Everyone must leave something behind when he dies, my grandfather said. A child or a book or a painting or a house or a wall built or a pair of shoes made. Or a garden planted. Something your hand touched some way so your soul has somewhere to go when you die. And when people look at that tree or that flower you planted, you're there. My grandfather said it doesn't matter what you do, so long as you change something from the way it was before you touched it into something that's like you after you take your hands away. The difference between the man who just cuts lawns and a real gardener is in the touching, he said. The lawn-cutter might just as well not have been there at all. The gardener will be there a lifetime."

Listening to him, I was in awe of the way his words flowed, and I was reminded of how poetic his writing was.

"Wow," I said. "You do have a gift."

"Well, thank you, but some people thought I was far too sentimental, you know."

"Really?"

"Oh, yes. I got letters from people, even other writers, who accused me of being too emotional and sentimental. But I believe in honest sentiment and the need to purge ourselves at certain times, which is ancient. Men would live at least five or six more years and not have ulcers if they could cry. The only good writing is intuitive writing. For years, I had a sign above my desk that said, 'Don't think.' Thinking is the enemy of good writing. You've got to write from your heart. It's the only way to tell a story and the only way a writer can ever truly connect with a reader."

"And I suspect that's what made your writing so great."

"I'd like to think so."

"But of course, not everyone can be a writer."

"Why not?"

"Not everyone has a gift like you had."

"That's bullshit."

I remembered hearing Bradbury could be earthy.

"Everyone should write. It's the only way to keep from going mad. You must stay drunk on writing so reality cannot destroy you. When you write, you fall in love, and out of that love, we remake the world. Love is the answer to everything."

I said nothing. I wanted to let that idea soak in.

"What about you?" he said. "I've been doing all the talking. Please tell me something about yourself. What kind of work do you do?"

"Well, my life isn't very glamorous, I'm afraid. I'm a software engineer."

"A software engineer," he said slowly, as if he were trying to understand it. "Do you like your work?"

"Actually, I do. I know it sounds boring, but I really like it."

"Then that's what you must do. You must do what you love and love what you do."

"I guess you're right," I said. "Sometimes I feel like a nerd. I mean some of my friends have such cool jobs. They have a lot of power and make a lot of money. My college roommate is on-track to be CEO of a big company. Nobody works for me, and I doubt I'll ever make much money."

"Then we have that in common," he said with a little laugh. "You don't write to get rich. My wife and I lived in the same little house for 50 years, a little yellow house in Cheviot Hills, a suburb of Los Angeles. That's where I wrote. I died in that house. Maggie and I raised our four daughters there. They took all the money I ever made. And you know what? I wouldn't have wanted it any other way."

I smiled. Yeah, this is the real Ray Bradbury, I thought, and I was so glad that somehow we had met.

"Well, it's been wonderful talking with you, Mr. Bradbury."

"Please call me Ray."

"Okay. I've got to tell you, Ray, I've found this conversation so refreshing."

"Me too. Will you do me a small favor?"

"Sure. What?"

"Tonight, before you go to bed, will you write something? It doesn't matter what it is. Just spend five minutes putting a bit of yourself down on a piece of paper, for no one but you."

"I'll be happy to do that."

"Good. It was a pleasure meeting you, Jason," he said, extending his hand.

"And you, Ray," I said, taking it. "Thank you."

"Take care," he said as I got up.

"You too."

I'd been in a funk, still coming out of the hard winter, I suppose. Ray had given me a lot to think about. He revived my spirit. I guess I'd been thinking of myself as more of a lawn-cutter than a gardener.

But really — a conversation with a dead man? Maybe I'd been dreaming the whole thing. Maybe he was just fantasy, I thought, like one of his stories.

Still, I felt grateful. I turned around to thank him again, but he was gone.

## How to Get Promoted

Fifteen years into my career, I was utterly bored. In the accounting firm where I worked, I'd gone as far as you can without making partner. I had no great desire to make partner, but I knew I wasn't a contender when a co-worker told me he overheard my boss say, "Alex isn't really partner material."

I thought about the prospect of staying where I was for another 15 years. The pay was okay, and I knew I could expect modest annual increases if I kept doing a reasonably good job. I was now getting stock options too. Of course, I wouldn't see that money until I retired. But knowing it would be waiting for me made it hard to quit.

But the monotony was killing me. It was harder and harder to come to work. After Covid, most accounting firms allowed their employees to work remotely. But our CEO was adamant that we all come into the office again.

I thought about going to work for another firm, but I knew I'd be hard-pressed to get as good a deal as I had. I was in the office 40 hours a week, but I probably really worked about 20. I'd learned how to look busy.

One day, I decided to call in sick, even though I wasn't. I just couldn't drag myself into the office. It was a warm and sunny morning, and I decided to play golf. My wife was at work, and my kids were at school. No one would know.

What a glorious morning. After nine holes, I was hitting just over par. At the turn, I ordered a hot dog and a beer and watched a little ESPN. I didn't mind if other golfers went ahead. The course wasn't crowded. Besides, I had all morning. Hell, I had most of the afternoon. In fact, after I finished 18, I had another beer before heading home.

When I got there, I went upstairs and brushed my teeth so Amanda wouldn't smell beer on my breath. When she got home with the kids, I was watching TV. She was surprised to see me.

"You're home early," she said. "Is everything okay?"

"Oh, yeah. Light day at work, so I decided to cut out early."

"Good for you. You work so hard."

I felt bad about lying. I almost fessed up just then, but I knew that would only invite questions. Besides, it was only one time.

Until the following Wednesday. I woke up early, dreading another dreary day at work. I waited until Amanda and the kids were gone, then called in sick.

Then I made a tee time for 10:00. I figured I could play 18 again and still get home before anyone else.

This time, though, when Amanda and the kids got home, I was sound asleep on the sofa. That second beer did me in.

"Are you okay?" Amanda said. "I mean you haven't missed a day of work in years, and now you've missed two days in two weeks."

"I'm fine," I said, sitting up. "A little stressed at work, that's all. I just needed a mental health day. I'm good now."

But at work, my absence hadn't gone unnoticed. The next day, a co-worker told me she'd heard my boss, Bill, asking someone if I was happy at the firm. Crap, I thought. I'm going to get fired.

But a couple of days later, Bill came into my office and gave me a five percent raise.

"I know you just got a raise," he said, "but the firm is doing well, and we want you to know you're really valued around here."

After Bill left, it occurred to me he might have thought I was going to leave. Maybe taking off got his attention.

So the following week, I called in sick and played golf again. This time, though, I waited until I knew Amanda and the kids were home before I got there.

"I thought maybe we could go out for dinner tonight," Amanda said with a smile. "After all, you're making the big bucks now."

At work, Bill wasn't the only one who noticed my absences. My employees were buzzing about it. Most of them were pissed off about having to come back into the office. Some of them took my absences as a sign they could work from home again, at least once in a while. I didn't give them permission. But they didn't ask. They just did it. But they also got their work done. Our clients seemed happy, and we maintained our billings. To me, that was all that really mattered.

In the meantime, more and more employees who worked for other managers at the firm were quitting, especially the younger ones. Employee turnover had been an issue at the firm for some time. Except on my team. Unlike my peers, I didn't push my employees. They were smart, and they'd figured out what it took to get by. Other managers frowned on that, but I was fine with it. I even encouraged it.

One day, I was having lunch with one of my employees, a young guy named Matt.

"Next time you play golf during the week," he said, "let me know, and I'll join you."

Damn! Somebody must have spotted me.

"It's okay," he said with a smile. "I won't say a word. I just thought we might talk about the Johnson account on the links instead of being chained to our desks."

The following week, Matt and I both called in sick. By the turn, we'd figured out a way to increase our billings with Johnson by at least five percent.

And so it went. Not everybody on my team played golf with me. But they all knew if they produced, they'd be okay, even if they took a "mental health day" once in a while or dressed down in the office.

"I don't really care how much or how little time you put in," I told my team. "Just maintain or grow your accounts. That's all you have to do."

Such laxity might have raised red flags with senior management. But senior management had bigger concerns. People on the other teams were quitting like crazy, and the productivity of those teams was way down. They even lost a few clients.

One day, Bill called me into his office.

"You know, Alex, I have to admit I was wrong about you," he said.

Diplomacy was not one of Bill's strengths.

"For a long time, I wasn't sure you were partner material here."

That hearsay was right, I thought.

"But your team is the only one growing billings, and your employee turnover is virtually nil. You're leading the way around here."

There was a knock at the door.

"Come in," Bill said.

The door opened, and in walked our CEO, Henry Pierce.

"I hope I haven't interrupted," he said.

"Not at all, Henry. I was just about to give Alex some very good news. Maybe you'd like to give it to him yourself."

"Indeed I would," Pierce said, unbuttoning his suit jacket and pulling up a chair.

"Alex, let me cut to the chase. You're doing a terrific job here, and we want to reward that. I'm delighted to tell you we're making you our newest partner. That comes with a 15 percent salary increase, and you'll now be on our bonus plan."

I was stunned. So this is what happens when you play hooky, I thought.

The following month, Pierce announced our employees could begin working from home again a few days a week and dressing casually in the office. He also announced our firm would begin offering free child care for employees and health insurance coverage for same-sex married couples.

As a result, far fewer of our employees left. Our business stabilized and began to grow again. And we began gaining a reputation for being a good place to work.

I arranged for a standing tee time on Wednesday mornings and told my team about it. They all wanted to join me. I had them take turns, three at a time. We talked business, came up with new ideas and solved problems on the links. During the cold weather months, four of us met on Wednesdays in art museums and coffee shops. We even went bowling.

I've decided to stay at my firm. I'm having a blast.

## Filling Gaps

It was at Parents Day at her pre-school when Brianna Cook first noticed her family was different. Most of the other kids in her class had a mom and a dad show up that day. Brianna's mom came by herself.

On the way home from school, Brianna said to her mom, "Mommy, do I have a dad?"

Jasmine Cook knew this day would come.

"Yes, you do," she said, looking at her daughter in her rear view mirror. "Let's talk about it when we get home."

As Brianna hung up her backpack, Jasmine got a drink of water. Her mouth was dry.

"Can I have a juice box?" Brianna said.

"Sure," Jasmine said, pulling one from the refrigerator and handing it to her daughter.

"Thanks."

Brianna went into the living room, climbed up on the sofa and sipped her juice. Jasmine came in and sat down beside her. She cleared her throat.

"Yes, Brianna, you have a dad," she said.

"Where is he?"

"I don't know."

"Why doesn't he live with us?"

"Brianna, your dad wasn't ready to be a daddy."

The little girl looked puzzled.

"Will he ever live with us?"

"No, Brianna."

She looked up at her mother. Jasmine hoped she wouldn't ask any more questions. What she had told her was true, but she didn't want to reveal any more of the truth just then, while her daughter was so young.

"Okay," Brianna said, sipping her juice and looking away. "Can I watch cartoons?"

"Sure."

Relieved, Jasmine grabbed the remote and turned on the TV.

In grade school, kids began to tease Brianna about not having a father. Their teasing hurt, and sometimes she would tell her mom.

"Please don't let them get to you," Jasmine would say. "They don't understand."

But the teasing did get to Brianna. It made her feel as though her family was in some way inferior. It made her feel she was somehow "less than" others.

She grew wary of others, even friends. How did she know that they wouldn't make fun of her too?

By junior high, though, as girls learned where babies come from and began to understand that some guys don't take responsibility for their actions, Brianna's friends stopped teasing her. A few even apologized for their hurtful remarks years earlier. Brianna was relieved, and she became more trusting.

She was also becoming more curious about her father. She began approaching her mom with more pointed questions.

*What was his name? What was he like? Where does he live? Why didn't he stay with you? Did you love him?*

Jasmine knew this day too would come. She was not eager to talk about it, but she knew Brianna, now a young teenager, had a right to know something about her father.

"His name was Anthony," she said. "He was a good man. He never hurt me, other than leaving me when I was pregnant with you. I wanted him to stay, but he wasn't ready for that."

"Did you love him?"

"Yes."

"Where is he?"

"I don't know."

But this was a half-truth. Jasmine may not have know exactly where Anthony was, but she knew he still lived nearby. She knew people who knew people who had stayed in touch with him.

Brianna didn't press further. She could see the discomfort on her mother's face. But she was glad to know her father was a good man, even if he did leave.

Brianna had been a pretty girl. By high school, she was blossoming into a beautiful young woman. Some of the boys her age began showing interest in her. Some said they just wanted to "hang out." She quickly learned what that really meant and cut these guys off.

Some boys, though, seemed genuinely interested in getting to know Brianna. But if she started to get close to one of these guys, Brianna would make him promise he wouldn't leave her.

Of course, no 16-year-old boy was going to make such a promise. But she was insistent. As a result, in high school, Brianna had lots of dates but never a boyfriend.

Just after her eighteen birthday, Brianna came home from school, grabbed a snack and went into the living room to wait for her mom to come home from work.

"Hi, Bri," Jasmine said as she came in.

"Hi."

Brianna sounded uptight.

"Is everything okay?" Jasmine said, hanging up her jacket.

"Yeah."

Jasmine came into the living room and kissed her daughter on her head. Then she held her face in her hands and said, "What's wrong?"

Brianna still wasn't sure how to say it, so she just blurted it out.

"I want to meet my father."

Jasmine was stunned even though she suspected this day too might come. She sat down next to her daughter.

"Why?"

"I'm not sure, Mama. It's just something I feel I need to do."

Brianna was looking down, but Jasmine's eyes were on her face, as if she were searching for some sign that her daughter was just kidding. But Brianna looked up with eyes wide open, waiting for a response.

"I don't know where your father is."

"But you can find him."

"That's true. If I really wanted to, I could probably find him."

"Mama, I love you, and I would never do anything to hurt you. But there's a gap in my life. I'm curious, Mama. I'm just curious. I want to meet him. I want to see what he looks like. I want to see if I can see myself in his face. I don't want to get to know him. I just want to see him, and I want him to know he has a daughter in this world who, thanks to you, is doing just fine. If I had a daughter who I'd never seen, I think I'd want to know that."

Jasmine reached out and took her daughter's hands.

"Oh, Bri," she said, beginning to cry. "I understand. I'll do what I can to find him."

Now Brianna was crying too.

"Thank you, Mama," she said, embracing her mother. "Thank you."

Brianna got to The Brew Box early. She hadn't been there before. She'd been in the inner city only a couple of times, and she wanted to make sure she could find the place and have her bearings when he came in.

But how would she recognize him? Her mother had never shown her a photograph of him or even described him. Maybe he would recognize Brianna because she looked like her mother. Or maybe Brianna would see herself in his face.

She ordered a cold brew coffee and sat down at a small table in the back of the coffee shop. It was late morning, and only a few people were in the place. At 11:00, a middle-aged man came in. She couldn't see his face well, but the sunlight through the big front window caught the gray in his hair.

He said something to the barista, as if he knew her. Then he looked around. It has to be him, Brianna thought. She stood up and slightly raised her hand.

He nodded and started toward her. He wore a loose-fitting jacket, a black T-shirt, blue jeans and work boots. As he came closer, she could see his face more clearly. It was thin, like Brianna's. His skin was dark, like hers, his jawline sharp, like hers.

Now just a few steps away, he said, "Brianna?"

Her heart was pounding. Her legs felt weak.

"Yes," she said.

"Good morning," he said with a small smile. "I'm Anthony."

He extended his hand. She took it. His handshake was firm.

"Thank you for reaching out," he said.

"Thank you for coming."

"Should we sit down?"

"Yes."

They sat down across from one another, both leaning back in their chairs.

"Would you like some coffee?" she said.

"No, thanks. I've already had some this morning."

Now she could see him clearly. His hair was a mix of black and gray. His eyes were puffy, with wrinkles at the corners. Small dark spots dotted his cheeks and nose. He looked older than her mother. She wondered if he was indeed older or if he had simply aged faster.

"I was surprised to hear from your mother after all this time," he said. "But I was happy to have the chance to finally meet you."

Brianna had so many questions. But she knew that wasn't the reason she had asked for this meeting.

"I reached out because I thought you might like to know I'm good. I'll be leaving for college this fall, and I wasn't sure we'd have this chance again. So I reached out."

His eyes glistened with tears.

"I'm sorry," he said, running his fingertips over his eyelids. "I'm sorry."

To Brianna, his tears were not unwelcome. Not that she was looking for a sign of remorse. But she was hoping her father was capable of showing emotion, that he was not cold-hearted.

"It's okay," she said.

He smiled.

"Look at you," he said. "Telling me it's okay. I should have been saying that to you all these years."

She sipped her coffee, unsure what else to say.

"I'm sorry I wasn't there for you," he said.

"Why?"

"Why what?"

"Why weren't you there for me? Why did you leave Mama?"

He looked down.

"I wasn't ready to be a father."

"But you *were* my father. You *are* my father."

"I was a scared kid, Brianna, not much older than you are now. I wasn't ready to be a husband or a father."

"And so you just left?"

"Yeah, I left."

Brianna hadn't intended to grill him. She had only wanted to meet him and let him know she was okay. She'd done that. It's time to go, she thought.

She drank down the last of her coffee and scooted her chair out.

"Brianna," he said.

"Yes?"

"We make choices. I've known for a long time that leaving your mother was a bad choice. I've regretted it every day since. But I've always hoped that bringing you into this world was a good choice. Now I see that it was. I'm proud of you, and I wish you much happiness."

"Thank you," she said.

She got up. He got up too. She thought about giving him a hug but couldn't bring herself to do that.

"Goodbye," she said.

"Goodbye, Brianna."

Walking away, she fought back tears. But when she got in her car, she started sobbing. She sat there crying for a long time before driving home.

Jasmine was sitting in the living room when Brianna got home. She could see her daughter had been crying.

"Are you okay?" she said.

"Yeah."

"Do you want to talk?"

"Yeah."

Brianna stepped into the living room, sat on the sofa next to mother and gave her a hug.

"I love you, Mama."

"I love you too."

"So, how did it go?"

"Well, I do kind of look like him," Brianna said with a small laugh.

"Yes, you do."

"And now he knows I'm okay."

"Good. I know that was important to you."

"And I think you were right."

"How so?"

"I don't think he was ready to be a father. Or a husband for that matter."

"No, he wasn't."

"Mama?"

"Yeah, baby?"

"Were you ready to be a mother?"

Jasmine smiled and reached out for Brianna's hand.

"Whether or not I was ready to be a mother, I've always felt blessed to be *your* mother."

"Thank you. Mama, he said something else."

"What?"

"He said he regrets leaving you."

"He did?"

"Yes. He said he's regretted it every day since he left you."

Now it was Jasmine's turn to cry. Brianna held her as she wept.

Finally, Jasmine wiped eyes.

"Are you okay?" Brianna said.

"Yeah. I am now."

"Why?"

"I did love your father, Bri. You were conceived in love. But as soon as I told him I was pregnant, he was gone, and I never knew how he felt about leaving like that. Now I know. Until today, you were feeling a gap in your life, and I was feeling a gap in mine too. Now, because of you, our gaps have been filled. So let's be happy, Bri. Let's move on and be happy."

## Lost and Found

Logan Beckett sat on the edge of his bed. His whole body was vibrating. He'd had two Cokes during his overnight shift. He'd drunk them to stay awake, but now he was regretting it. He was tired but knew he couldn't fall asleep now.

He was tempted to get online. But what would he do? Doom scroll all morning? Maybe I should go for a bike ride, he thought. That'll wear me out.

When he was a kid, Logan used to ride with his dad on a nearby bike trail. When Logan was a teenager, his dad gave him his bike. It was a basic road bike, not built for speed, but Logan was not in a hurry.

His life had become a slow-motion do-loop. Stock shelves at Target from 11:00 p.m. until 7:00 a.m., six days a week. Come home, eat breakfast, fall asleep until mid-afternoon, eat lunch, go online, play video games, watch something on Netflix, eat dinner, get ready for work. This had been Logan's routine for two years now, since he'd graduated from high school.

Maybe I should be grateful, he thought. After all, his parents were charging him only $100 a month for rent. His mother had given him her old car. He had a job, a car, a TV, a laptop, decent clothes and a place a live. He'd saved about 20 grand. What more did he need?

How about a reason to live? Was his purpose in life to stock shelves? How about an *interesting* job? How about some friends? Logan hardly ever saw anyone his age anymore. The other guys stocking shelves were older. They had families. Even the overnight security guard had a family, two kids, who she talked about all the time.

And how about a girlfriend? Logan never talked to young women anymore. What young woman would want to talk to him? He didn't go to college. He worked all night, slept all day and lived in his parents' basement. Some catch he was.

Sometimes Logan felt life wasn't worth living. More than once, he'd actually thought about ending it all. Maybe I should go down to the bike trail, ride away and not come back, he thought. Who would even care?

Logan attached his dad's old bike rack to the back of his car and strapped down his bike. Driving to the trail, he thought of the times he and dad used to ride there, when his dad still spent time with him.

Logan was small then, and they didn't go very far. Now as he parked, he saw a sign for Milford, eight miles to the south. He wasn't sure he could make it that far but figured he could always turn back.

As Logan began pedaling, his legs hurt. They were used to lifting, not stretching. His bike wobbled. He was afraid he might fall over. Maybe this wasn't such a good idea, he thought.

But within a few minutes, his bike began to feel familiar again. He was still going slow, but his bike was steady now, and his legs had settled into an easy rhythm.

It was early May. The air was brisk. The trees had leafed out, patches of small, yellow flowers lined the trail and the river, just below, was high. Logan hadn't been out in nature in a long time. He'd almost forgotten how beautiful this place was.

As sunlight streamed through the canopy of trees, Logan realized how much he had missed the sun. These days most of his waking hours were artificially lit. He'd grown used to an indoor world, a world of boxes and shelves, of video games and movies, of social media posts and TikTok dancers. He'd lost touch with the real world. He'd almost forgotten the feel of the warm sun on his face.

"Milford 6" read a sign. Had he ridden two miles already? Maybe he'd be able to go all the way after all.

But what if he didn't have the energy to make it back? By then, it might be late morning, which was like the middle of the night for him. He peddled on. He would take his chances.

When he finally reached a sign that said Milford, Logan looked around and realized the town lay just below. It was an old town whose main street was lined with shops and restaurants. He'd been there once with his parents. Now he was thirsty and decided to go into the town to get something to drink.

He descended a winding path, crossed a bridge over the river and looked for a place to get a bottle of water. He spotted a coffee shop called Revival and parked his bike outside. He didn't have a lock but doubted anyone would steal it.

Logan stepped inside.

"Good morning," said a middle-aged woman behind the counter.

"Good morning," he said.

The shop was small. There were no overhead lights, only lamps, which gave the place a warm glow. People sat across from one another at several tables. A young guy was on his laptop, wearing earbuds. An older woman sat alone, reading a book. Of all the customers, only she seemed to notice Logan.

He stepped up to the counter and ordered a bottle of water. Having paid, he turned to leave and noticed the older woman was still looking at him — and smiling. He nodded and left.

On his way back, Logan kept thinking of that woman. Why was she looking at him? Did he know her? Maybe she smiled at everyone, he thought.

By the time he got home, Logan was famished and exhausted. He wolfed down a bowl of cereal and a donut, went downstairs and fell into a deep sleep.

That morning, Barb Langley had pulled on a sweater, grabbed a book and headed out her front door. She then walked three blocks to Revival for coffee, as she did nearly every morning.

Sometimes she thought about selling her house. It was old and, these days, always in need of repair. She'd lived there for 40 years. Maybe it's time to downsize, she thought.

She hadn't thought about moving when she was working. She couldn't imagine living anywhere else, even after Bob died and the kids had moved away. She could walk to work, and the house was paid off. Now, though, she was alone, and managing the house and the yard by herself had become a real challenge.

Reaching Main Street, Barb still had to resist her old habit of turning left to go the library, where she had worked for 31 years. Were it not for the policy of mandatory retirement at 65, she'd still be working there. She loved her job. It had given her a sense of purpose.

Barb turned right on the cobblestone sidewalk and went into Revival. She was sipping her coffee and enjoying her book when she noticed a young man come through the door. He reminded her of a younger version of her son Matt.

She missed Matt and her daughter Ashley too. After college, they'd both moved out. Ashley went to the West Coast, Matt to the East Coast. Ashley was now married. She and her husband were both totally devoted to their careers and had decided not to have children. Matt always seemed to have a new girlfriend but never a fiancé.

Now looking at the young man at the counter reminded Barb how long it had been since she'd seen either of her children. Raising them, she never imagined they would be apart.

But here she was, not only alone but feeling lost. She had been a wife, a mother and a librarian. Now she had nothing to do but sip coffee, read books and tend her garden. No one wrote her or stopped by anymore. Once in a while, Ashley called. Matt rarely called. Barb was grateful they both visited at Christmastime. But the rest of the year, she was alone.

Now she allowed herself, for a moment, to imagine this young man was her son, that Matt was near her again. The very idea made her smile.

Two weeks later, Logan decided to bike to Milford again. He'd just gotten home from work. He was tired, but the monotony of his life was driving him crazy. He needed a break.

This time, the morning was much warmer, and by the time Logan got to Milford, he was parched. Once again, he parked his bike outside of Revival and went in for some water.

The place was packed, with a lot more young people this time. School must be out, Logan thought. Waiting in line, he looked around and saw the older woman he had seen before. Again, she was sitting alone, looking his way and smiling.

Logan paid for his bottle of water and looked around again. The woman was still looking at him. He didn't want to be rude, but he had to know why. He stepped over to her table to find out.

"Good morning," he said.

"Good morning," she said.

"You look familiar. Have we met?"

"You look familiar too. I'm Barb Langley," she said, extending her hand.

"Logan Beckett," he said, taking it.

"You've been here before," she said.

"Yes, once, a couple of weeks ago. I think I saw you then."

"Well, I didn't mean to stare, but you look a great deal like my son. When he was younger."

"I'll take that as a compliment," Logan said with a small smile.

"Oh, yes! He's quite handsome."

"Well, it's nice to meet you."

Just as Logan began to turn away, Barb said, "May I buy you a cup of coffee?"

"Thanks, but I just got off work. I work at night. I need to get some rest."

"Decaf?"

Maybe it was the plaintive way she said that or the sadness in her eyes or his own feeling of loneliness, but Logan said, "Okay."

She walked back over to the counter with him and bought his coffee.

Sitting across from Barb at the table, Logan thought, she really does look familiar. She reminded him a slightly younger version of his grandmother.

"Thanks for this," he said, sipping his coffee. "It's good."

They briefly introduced themselves. Neither of them even hinted they were lonely. They didn't have to. Sometimes the things clearest about people are unspoken.

"Do you think you'll ride your bike down here again?" Barb said.

"Yeah. You know, the first time, I wasn't sure I could make it. I hadn't ridden a bike in a long time. But I didn't really have any trouble, and it's great to be outdoors. I'm thinking about coming back next week."

Barb smiled.

"Do you like to read books?" she said.

"I haven't read a book since high school. But, yeah, I like to read."

"How about the next time you're here, I give you a tour of the library? It's right down the street."

"I'd like that."

They agreed to meet at Revival the following Wednesday morning, grab coffee, then walk down to the library.

The following Wednesday, Barb stopped in front of the library door and took a deep breath.

"You okay?" Logan said.

"Yes. It's just that I haven't been back here since I retired. It's kind of a strange feeling."

"We don't have to go in."

"It's okay."

She pulled open the door, and he followed her inside.

"Barb!" a pretty young woman behind the front desk called out softly.

Barb smiled and stepped over to her, and they embraced.

"Hello, Isa. How are you?"

"I'm fine. And you?"

"I'm well, thanks."

Then Barb remembered she was with Logan.

"Isa Delgado, I'd like you to meet my friend, Logan Beckett. I've offered to give him a tour of the library this morning."

"Good morning," Logan said.

"Good morning," Isa said with a smile.

Looking back at Barb, Isa said, "Things haven't changed much around here, but let me know if you have any questions."

"Thank you. I will."

Then turning to Logan, Barb said, "This way."

He followed her past rows of bookshelves. She paused a couple of times but kept going until they reached a cozy alcove with two cushioned armchairs.

"Let's sit for a minute," she said.

"Okay."

Sitting down, he looked over at her, uncertain what was happening.

"I'm sorry," she said. "It just feels a little surreal being here."

"I'll bet. You spent a big part of your life here."

"It's not just that."

"What is it then?"

"I loved this place. I loved the books, and I loved the people I worked with. I guess —"

"What?"

"Well, I guess I expected a bigger send-off."

Logan looked puzzled.

"Oh, I know that must sound petty. But after 30 years, I would have thought there might have been a dinner or something. On my last day, someone brought in cupcakes. That was it."

"I'm sorry."

"That's why I haven't been back, Logan. I thought it might be fun to show you this place. But now that I'm here, I don't feel like I belong here anymore."

Barb looked like she could cry.

"Ray Bradbury," Logan said.

"What?"

"Where can I find a book by Ray Bradbury?"

"Are you serious?"

"Yes."

"Okay," she said, getting up. "Follow me."

She led him to the fiction section, where the books were organized by author.

"Here are Bradbury's books. Do you like him?"

"I remember reading a book by him in high school."

"*Fahrenheit 451*?"

"Yeah."

"Everybody reads that one. Do you like science fiction?"

"Sure."

"Have you read *The Martian Chronicles*?"

"No."

Barb leaned in, squinted her eyes and ran her index finger across the spines until she found it.

"Here you go," she said, handing him a hardback book with a red cover.

"Thanks."

"Bradbury was a great writer. He learned to write by reading books in libraries, you know."

"I didn't know that."

"Yes, he never went to college."

Not wanting Logan to get the wrong impression, she quickly added, "Not that you should go to college."

He smiled.

"Did you go?" he said.

"Yes, and I worked in the library on campus. That's where I met my husband. Going to college changed my life."

Then she added, "I've heard that Target pays for college tuition for its employees."

"Yeah, I remember someone mentioning that. But I don't know if I'm cut out for college."

"Why not?"

He didn't really have a good answer. He had been an average student. In truth, he had thought about going to college, but no one had ever encouraged him to go, not even his parents. They didn't seem to expect much from him anymore. Logan didn't expect much of himself anymore.

But now Barb looked at him, waiting for an answer.

"I'll look into it," he said.

"Good."

Barb looked around the library. She had a wistful look in her eyes. Logan sensed she missed this place.

"Have you ever thought about volunteering here?"

In truth, she had thought about volunteering there, even though she was still felt bad about her send-off. But now she thought about how friendly Isa had been that morning. Maybe she'd harbored hard feelings long enough.

"I'll give it some thought," she said.

"Good."

"Anything else you'd like to see?"

"No, thanks. I guess I'd better get going."

"Okay. Would you like me to check that book out for you?"

"That'd be great," he said, handing it back to her.

Isa was still at the front desk. She scanned Barb's card and the book and handed them back along with a receipt.

"It's so good to see you again, Barb," she said. "I hope you'll come back in soon."

Then, looking at Logan, she smiled and said, "Both of you."

Logan smiled too.

Out on the sidewalk, he said, "Thanks for the tour ... and the book."

"My pleasure. I know you must be tired. Thanks for staying awake a little longer."

They shook hands and said goodbye. Logan got on his bike and tucked the book under his arm. He had no other way to carry it. But as he rolled down the pedestrian ramp and into the street, the book slid out from under his arm and fell onto the pavement. He stopped and bent down to pick it up.

A car coming toward him wasn't slowing down. Logan didn't see it, but Barb did. She waved her arms and screamed, "Stop!"

The driver looked up and slammed on his brakes. His car screeched to a stop just in time. He got out to make sure Logan was okay. Logan's bike had tipped over, but he was unhurt. He picked up his bike and walked it back up to the sidewalk.

"Why don't we sit down for a minute?" Barb said, motioning to a bench.

Logan parked his bike, and they sat down.

"That was a close one," Barb said.

"Sure was. You probably saved my life."

"Well, I don't know about that ..."

"Thank you."

Then Logan said, "When I go in tonight, I'm going to ask about the tuition plan."

"Good. And I'm going to start volunteering at the library."

"Good."

Taking a deep breath, Logan said, "Well, I guess I'd better get going."

They both got up. Turning toward Logan, Barb opened her arms, and they embraced.

"Take care of yourself," she said.

"You too."

When the street was clear, Logan walked his bike across, then tucked the book snugly under his arm and headed home. For the first time in a long time, he felt hopeful about his future.

Barb watched to make sure Logan got off okay, then began to walk home. For the first time in a long time, she felt she still had something to give.

## The Bargain

Camping in the Bob Marshall Wilderness for a few days had seemed like a good idea. In Montana, it's still winter in mid-March, and many of Aidan Hensley's classmates headed south for spring break. But Aidan drove two hours north to "The Bob," a million-acre preserve that straddles the Continental Divide. When other zigged, Aidan zagged.

He'd left his car at the Benchmark trailhead and hiked east into the park along a pass through the mountains. At that point, the snow was only a few inches deep, and the trail was easy to see. He hiked all afternoon, then pitched his tent in the forest, built a fire and ate a protein bar and an apple for dinner.

In the morning, Aidan was awakened by wind whipping through the trees. He poked his head out of his tent, and the frigid air stung his face. The forest floor was now coated with snow. He was tempted to build a fire but decided to get moving.

He lowered a nylon bag with his food from a rope he'd rigged up between two trees to keep it away from any wild animals overnight. He wolfed down a banana and a hard-boiled egg, took down his tent, stuffed it and his sleeping bag in his backpack and hiked out.

Through the morning, the snow fell harder, and the wind grew fierce. By noontime, the trail was obscured by a layer of fresh snow. Behind him, even his footprints were gone.

Aidan knew he needed to find cover. He thought he saw trees in the distance and wearily trudged toward them.

"Hey, you forgot your phone," Aidan's roommate Ethan said as Aidan was about to head out.

"I'm leaving it," Aidan said. "I'm on break."

"Suit yourself."

Aidan now regretted that choice. He knew the weather in Montana could be dicey in March, but he was so sure of himself as a hiker that he hadn't bothered to check out the forecast or bring a compass.

Most of the time, Aidan's self confidence worked for him. But sometimes, it was really arrogance and got him in trouble. This was quickly becoming one of those times.

On his second day in the wilderness, Aidan had hunkered down, hoping the snowstorm would pass. But in the morning, he was jarred awake by fierce wind. He poked his head out of his tent. It had to be below zero. He couldn't imagine hiking in this. He decided to stay put and build a fire.

Once he got a fire going, Aidan lowered his nylon bag and pulled out a protein bar and an orange. He was alarmed when he realized he hadn't packed more food. He guessed he had enough for just a couple more days.

He dragged a log over and sat close to the fire. He wasn't sure what he should do next. He could venture out and try to find a trail, but he knew his chances were slim.

He was lost, and who would even know where to look for him? Only Ethan knew he was going to The Bob. He hadn't even told his parents.

Maybe the best he could do was keep a fire going so anyone who might be looking for him would see the smoke. He gathered logs and placed a few more on the fire. He hoped they were dry enough to burn but wet enough to give off plenty of smoke.

Aidan was used to getting his way, but now he was stuck. He felt powerless.

Shivering, he reflected on his situation and realized he might not make it. For the first time in years, Aidan thought of God. As a boy, he went to church with his parents. But by the time he was a teenager, he'd stopped believing in God.

Now, desperate for help, he allowed for the possibility that he'd been wrong. If God does exist, he thought, maybe he'd be open to a bargain.

What could he offer God? To change, he thought. To treat people better.

Aidan thought about how he had treated women. He had the looks and smooth way of talking that attracted women. But he had never had a real relationship because the only thing he cared about was getting women into bed.

It had worked, but he knew in his heart it was wrong. *Let me live, God, and I'll treat women with respect.*

Aidan thought about how little he shared. Why hadn't he told his parents he was taking this trip? Because he thought they'd disapprove? No, because he liked to keep people guessing. He liked being a man of mystery.

But look where mystery had gotten him. *Let me live, God, and I'll be more open.*

He thought more about his parents. They so wanted a college education for him that they were willing to draw from their savings to cover the cost. They even bought him a car. Aidan could have chipped in. Instead, he took full advantage of his parents' generosity.

Now, though, he thought maybe he should go to work in the summer to at least help pay for his tuition. *Let me live, God, and I'll go to work this summer.*

He thought about his group projects at school. He never did his fair share, and he always had excuses. *Let me live, God, and I'll do my part.*

As darkness fell, Aidan reached into his nylon bag and pulled out some beef jerky. The only food left was a couple of protein bars.

He tossed the bag back up over his rope line for the night. He knew The Bob was full of grizzlies and black bears. Maybe they're still hibernating, he thought. He could have easily found out before he left, but he didn't want to make the effort.

Aidan had become lazy. He put things off. He avoided making choices. That's why, even as he was about to complete his sophomore year in college, he still hadn't declared a major. *Let me live, God, and I'll get serious about school.*

If he did these things, would that be enough for God? Thinking about that, and the cold, made his head hurt. He decided to get some sleep.

In the morning, he built up the fire, hoping someone would see the smoke, but his hope was beginning to fade.

Maybe I'm kidding myself, he thought. It certainly wouldn't be his first act of deception. Aidan lied all the time, and he lied easily. It was a way for him to get what he wanted and gain an upper hand.

But now the only one he was fooling was himself, and nature had the upper hand.

*Let me live, God, and I'll be honest.*

He was famished. He lowered his nylon sack and grabbed one of the two remaining protein bars. He wondered how long he could survive on one protein bar.

A light snow was now falling, and he decided to venture out into a clearing to see if he could get his bearings.

His only way of telling time or gauging direction was by where the sun was in the sky. It was now nearly directly overhead.

Looking around, Aidan realized he was in a valley surrounded by mountains. During his hike in, the terrain had been relatively flat. He'd come in from the west. He figured if he knew which way was west, he could head there and try to find his way out. He would come back in a little while to gauge west by the afternoon sun.

Back at his campsite, he placed a few more logs on the fire and sat down to warm himself. He thought of Ethan and his other classmates sunning themselves in Florida. *What's wrong with me? Why did I come out here by myself, without a phone? Why I am such a loner?* Why was he a manipulator? Why was he a liar? Where had he gone wrong?

Aidan had never felt comfortable with self reflection. He thought of it as navel gazing. But now, alone, with nothing to do and the real prospect of dying in this wilderness, maybe it was time to think about why he was the way he was and, if he still had time, to change his ways.

He noticed the sunlight hitting the trees at an angle and made his way back out to the clearing. Now the sun hovered over a mountain range, and he knew that was west. He extended his arm and pointed in that direction and stood there, pointing west, like the needle of a compass.

Tomorrow he would head that way, looking for a pass through the mountains, hoping he might find the trail or at least a sign. He lowered his arm but stood there a few more minutes, looking at the mountains, imagining his hike in the morning and saying a prayer for his salvation.

In the middle of the night, Aidan was awakened by a noise outside his tent. It was the sound of fabric ripping and paper tearing. He heard the scratching of the claw of an animal against the ground, then chomping.

*My protein bar! Crap!* He'd forgotten to hang up his nylon bag that afternoon, and an animal, probably a bear, had found it.

Aidan lay still, hoping the beast would go away. He heard it moving around, sniffing. He heard a grunt, then twigs and branches snapping. The sound got fainter and fainter. Whatever it was, it was leaving. Then there was silence.

Aidan lay still, unable to go back to sleep, and said a silent prayer of thanksgiving.

He was awakened by the morning light. He unzipped the tent and looked outside, half expecting to see a bear. Instead, he saw his nylon bag, ripped apart, and bear tracks all around.

It was freezing, and he was tempted to build up the fire, but he wanted to get going, so he packed everything up and headed out to the clearing. He looked west at the mountains, then closed his eyes and asked God to help him find his way.

Aidan hiked all morning, searching for a trail, but the snow was deep, and there was no sign of a trail. By midday, he was exhausted. He felt like stopping and setting up camp, but he knew if he did that, he might not have the strength to resume hiking. So he pressed on.

Nothing looking familiar, yet he knew he was heading in the right direction. The trail he had taken into the park had been fairly straight, and he hadn't strayed very far north or south. He hoped hiking due west would eventually lead him back to the Benchmark trailhead.

Aidan again said a silent prayer for guidance. It's funny, he thought. A few days ago, he didn't think God existed. Now he was imploring him. Maybe God was an invention of his desperate mind. Maybe he was deluding himself. But as he followed the sun in the cloudless sky, he had faith that God was not only real but that he was leading him home.

He thought about the bargains he had struck with God when he'd lost his way. Now the idea of bargaining with God seemed wrong. Aidan felt bad about how he had treated people, and he wanted to treat them better because he knew they deserved respect, not because he had struck a deal with God. He wanted to be honest because lying felt wrong. He wanted to go to work that summer not because he owed God anything but because he wanted to help out his parents, whom he loved.

I'm navel gazing, he thought. *Maybe so. If I am, it's about time. It's about time to start living right, even if I don't make it.*

He had hiked all day, and the sun was getting low in the sky. He felt weak. He could no longer bear the weight of his backpack, so he slipped it off, and it fell into the snow. If he had to hunker down for the night, he would try to find trees and take shelter, but he would go there unencumbered.

He looked up at the mountains ahead. They were no longer a seamless range. They were divided to his left and right, and he realized he was hiking on a pass between them.

"Aidan!"

He tried to locate the source of the voice. He turned around full circle, searching the landscape. He wanted to wave his arms but couldn't lift them. He simply had nothing left. He felt empty, like a well run dry.

But then he saw the silhouettes of several people in the distance, directly below the setting sun, and knew he was saved.

"Thank you," he whispered.

Then he fell to his knees.

## Reset

Twenty-year-old Carlos Martinez looked out the window of the bedroom he still shared with his two brothers and watched kids popping out of a school bus at the street corner. He remembered the joy of coming home like that, of his mother greeting him as he got off the school bus. Where had the time gone?

His life was a blur, and yet lately it also felt like it was standing still. Every day was the same. Wake up in the early afternoon. Go downstairs and get something to eat. Go back upstairs and get online and play video games for the rest of the afternoon. Get something else to eat. Sometimes draw in his sketchbook. Take a nap. Wake up again, shower and go to work — the overnight shift at the Chevron food mart down the street — as his family was getting ready for bed.

Carlos barely talked with anyone anymore. His old friends were now in college or working day jobs. The only people he "talked with" these days were customers, strangers online or his mom.

Carlos hadn't been outside his neighborhood in months. He didn't drive or date. Who would want to date a loser like me, he wondered.

The tedium was wearing him down, but he didn't know what else to do. The only thing that had ever really interested him was drawing, but he knew he couldn't make a living "doodling," as his dad called it.

At work, when the cash register was full of bills, Carlos had to take the money out and put it in a safe in the floor behind the checkout counter. He usually did this near the end of his shift.

One night, when he had just clocked in, Carlos noticed the cash register was packed with bills. The store was empty, and he decided to go ahead and put the money in the safe. Just as he was opening it, he heard a buzz. Someone had come in. He placed the bills in the vault but decided to get up to see who had come in before closing it.

A man, wearing a ski mask and holding a gun, stepped quickly up the counter.

"Give me all that money!" he said, pointing the gun at Carlos.

"It's in a safe in the floor," Carlos said, his heart pounding.

"Bullshit! I just saw you take out a bunch of bills!" he said, waving his gun. "Now give them to me!"

Carlos tried to stay calm. He wished someone else would walk in.

"Okay," he said. "I'll need to bend down and get the money out of the safe."

The man leaned over the counter.

"You do that. And don't try to pull anything."

There was an emergency button under the counter, but Carlos knew if he pushed it, the man would see him. So he got down on one knee and pulled the bills out of the safe. Then he stood up and handed them over.

The man stuffed them into his jacket pocket.

"Put your hands up," he said.

Carlos raised his hands. The man laughed. Then he shot Carlos in the chest.

Carlos cried out, staggered for a moment, then fell to the floor.

Two days later, Carlos woke up. He heard beeping, opened his eyes and looked around. He realized he was lying in bed in a hospital room. When he tried to move, a sharp pain shot through his chest. He moaned loudly.

A nurse came into his room.

"Hello, Mr. Martinez," she said.

"Where am I?"

"You're at UNM Hospital. I'm your nurse this shift. My name is Jaime," she said, checking a device next to the head of his bed.

"What happened?"

"You were shot in the chest, but you're very lucky. The bullet just missed your heart. You had to have open-heart surgery. It was successful."

Carlos remembered the man in the food mart and getting shot but nothing after that.

"How long will I be here?"

"About a week. Then you'll probably go to rehab."

"Are my parents here?"

"Your mom is downstairs having lunch. She should be back soon. She's been here a lot. She'll be thrilled you're awake. How's your pain?"

"My chest hurts like hell when I try to move."

"That's to be expected. If you like, we can give you something for the pain."

"I'm okay. Thanks."

He heard someone at the door.

"You're awake!" his mother exclaimed.

"Yes, Mrs. Martinez," Jaime said. "He just woke up."

"Hi, Mom."

She rushed over to his bed, bent down and kissed him on the forehead.

"It's so good to see you awake. How do you feel?"

"Okay. Just sore."

"I'll leave you two alone," Jaime said. "If you need anything, just page me."

"Thank you," Carlos' mother said.

She pulled over a chair and sat down next to the bed.

"What happened, Mom?"

"Someone robbed your store and shot you."

"Who?"

"We don't know. Whoever it was, he got away, at least for now. But the whole thing was recorded. Clips are all over the news and social media. The police think they'll find the guy eventually."

"I think he'd been watching me. He knew I'd just taken money out of the cash register and was putting it in the safe."

"You were just doing your job. Chevron's been great. They even started a GoFundMe campaign to raise money to cover your medical bills. They're going to be steep."

"I'm sorry, Mom."

"Oh, honey. Don't worry. We'll get by. The most important thing is that you're okay. Your doctor told me it's a miracle that bullet didn't kill you. It just missed your heart."

"How long will it take me to heal?"

"At least a month."

"The nurse told me I might need to go to a rehab facility."

"Well, that all depends on your condition when you leave here. We'd love to have you come straight home."

"But where would I stay? I don't think I'll be able to go upstairs for a while."

"You can stay in the family room. We'll set it up for you."

Carlos looked at his mother. Her face looked drawn. She looked older. He knew this must be so hard on her, especially with three other kids to look after at home.

"Are you doing okay?"

"Yes," she said, patting his hand. "It was a shock when we learned you'd been shot. A policeman came to the house. I guess they didn't want to call. Everyone was in bed. Dad answered the door. At that point, we didn't know your condition. Dad and I rushed here. A few hours later, a doctor told us you were going to be okay. Dad went home. I slept here. I've been here as much as I could the past couple of days. I'm so relieved you're going to be okay."

"You should go home and get some rest. I'll be fine."

"Are you sure?"

"Yes."

"Well, okay. Dad will be by after work. I'll come back tomorrow."

"Mom, the kids need you. Stay home and take care of yourself. Please."

She smiled.

"Okay. The kids will be home from school soon. But if you need me for anything, just call."

"I will, Mom. Thanks."

"I love you, Carlos."

"I love you too."

That evening, Carlos' father came to visit.

"Hi, Dad," Carlos said as he stepped into the room.

"Buenas noches."

His father sometimes fell back on Spanish when he was anxious. He was still wearing his work clothes, which were dirty and wet with sweat. Even from halfway across the room, Carlos could smell him. In such a sanitary environment, he seemed very out-of-place.

"You're lucky," he said.

Carlos gave him a puzzled look.

"That you weren't killed."

"Yeah."

"I guess going to church paid off."

Carlos got the dig. His father, mother, sister and brothers went to Mass every Sunday. Carlos stopped going after he graduated from high school. That didn't sit well with his father, especially given Carlos was still living at home.

"Maybe so," Carlos said.

"Chevron's raising funds for your medical care."

"Yeah, Mom told me. That's great."

"It's important. The hospital bill is going to be huge."

"I can imagine."

"You know you can't go back to working at that gas station. It's too dangerous."

"I'm not sure what else to do."

"Well, you're going to have some time to think about that. Maybe it's time to go to college."

His father hadn't gone to college. Since his kids were little, he'd told them all he wanted them to go to college. Carlos had thought about it, but he was an average student and didn't like school.

"I'll think about it," Carlos now said, wanting to change the subject.

"Good."

After an awkward silence, his father said, "Do you need anything?"

"No, I think I'm all set here."

There was a knock at the door.

"Dinner," said an aide, carrying a tray.

"Come in," Carlos said.

His father stepped out of the way.

"Have you had dinner yet?" Carlos said to his father.

"Not yet. I'll eat when I get home."

"Well, I'm sure you're hungry, and Mom's probably waiting. Thanks for stopping by."

"Okay. I'll see you later."

"See you, Dad."

Then, without even a handshake, his father left.

Carlos healed fast. After his hospital stay, he spent less than a week in rehab before being sent home. On the morning of his discharge, his mom picked him up and brought him home. As promised, the family room had been transformed into a sort of bedroom.

"Wow!" he said, stepping into the room.

Carlos no longer needed to use a walker, but the rehab facility had sent him home with one, just in case.

The GoFundMe campaign had raised nearly $100,000 to cover Carlos' medical expenses, well above average for such campaigns. Carlos' campaign was boosted by periodic news stories and social media posts about his assailant still being on the loose.

Carlos' father was right: Carlos' medical bill was huge. Fortunately, Chevron's health insurance covered most of the cost. With the GoFundMe campaign, there was actually money left over. By rights, Chevron could have kept it, but they gave it to Carlos.

"The boys got your bed down here," his mother said.

"And my desk."

It was next to a large window, facing out.

"Yes, they brought that down too. I thought you might want to draw there."

His mother had always encouraged his artwork. She had bought him sketchbooks and art supplies since he was a boy. Carlos had given up on his father being supportive.

The family room was small, but it was much roomier than his bedroom. For the next month or so, Carlos would have his own recliner, sofa and TV. For the first time he could remember, he would have his own bedroom.

He had lunch with his mother in the kitchen. He seldom ate a meal with anyone anymore. It was nice to have someone to talk to.

"Well, I need to run some errands," she said when they were finished. "The kids will be home in a few hours. Will you be okay here on your own?"

"I'll be fine, Mom. Thanks."

"Are you feeling okay?"

"Yes."

"Any pain?"

"Just a little soreness when I move around."

"Okay. Don't overdo it. Just call if you need anything."

"I will."

When his mother had left, Carlos sat in the recliner and leaned back. The house was quiet, and he realized it was the first time he'd been alone there for a very long time. He took a sip of the lemonade his mother had made him. It was so good to be home. He looked around the room, now his room. I could get used to this, he thought.

His mother had placed his sketchbook and a tall coffee mug filled with drawing pencils on his desk. Carlos got up, slowly stepped over to it and sat down.

Through the window, he had a full view of the backyard. It was small but immaculate, kept that way by his father, who insisted on doing all the yard work himself. Carlos had asked to cut the grass many times, but his father wouldn't hear of it.

So once Carlos asked his mother instead.

"Oh, no. Dad would never let anyone else cut the grass."

"Why?"

"No one else could ever cut it as well as he can. At least that's what he thinks."

Whatever the reason, his father's refusal to allow him to cut the grass or take on other "grown up" tasks around the house left Carlos feeling his father didn't trust him.

Right below the family room window was his mother's large flower garden. It was late spring, and most of the flowers were in bloom. As a boy, Carlos loved those flowers. His mother had taught him their names, and he sometimes worked in the garden with her.

Now he opened his sketchbook to a blank page and selected a sharpened charcoal pencil. He studied the flowers for a few minutes, then lightly moved the pencil tip across the page. He drew the outline of the flowerbed first, then filled it in with poppies, irises, pansies, peonies and tulips.

He wanted to paint them too, but his watercolors were still upstairs. He wasn't ready to climb stairs, so he'd have to wait until someone could go up and get them.

He was tempted to take a little nap. Even after several weeks of not working, he was still transitioning from his old routine.

At the corner of his desk lay his laptop computer. It was even plugged into the wall outlet. But he had no interest in going online. During his recovery, he'd actually *thought about* going online and not done so automatically, and he realized his computer had little to offer that really interested him.

What *did* interest him he hadn't been sure. But now, looking down at his drawing, he knew what it was. He'd always loved art, and he was excited about the prospect of drawing and painting during his recuperation.

After a few weeks, Carlos was nearly healed. He'd filled two sketchbooks with drawings and created half a dozen paintings, including a now full-color version of his mother's garden.

His favorite thing to paint was the Sandia Mountains in the distance, especially when they took on a red hue at sunset. *Sandia* means watermelon in Spanish, and some of Carlos' watercolors almost looked edible.

As she always had, his mother praised his artwork, and his brothers and sister checked out his new creations every day. His father, though, stayed his distance. He seldom came into the family room anymore, and he showed no interest in Carlos' art.

His recuperation coming to an end, Carlos knew he needed to decide what to do next. He'd just turned 21. He was now an adult. He knew he couldn't live at home much longer.

Chevron had offered him a position as an assistant store manager, a step up from his old cashier job with an opportunity to get into management with a large company. His father encouraged him to consider it, but Carlos had no interest.

From his reimmersion in art, he was sure he wanted to become an artist. He knew he had natural talent. But he also knew that, to become an artist, he'd need training. Aside from his art classes in high school, he'd never had any formal training, and he knew little about the world of art. If he was going to become an artist, he wanted to get some exposure to real artists.

So he decided to go to an art school. He checked out what the University of New Mexico had to offer, but in-state tuition was more than $23,000 a year. If he enrolled there, he'd burn through his GoFundMe money in a year.

A better option, he thought, was Santa Fe Community College, which offered a two-year art degree. Annual tuition was only $2,500, so modest he'd have enough to also afford an apartment in Santa Fe for two years.

Of course, there was also the plus of Santa Fe itself. It was a creative arts hotbed. And it was an hour closer to Taos, where many artists lived.

He'd been to Santa Fe. It was an hour away. His parents had taken the family there several times when Carlos was growing up. They even spent the night once. It was the closest thing to a family vacation they ever had.

Even as a boy, Carlos had loved the vibe in Santa Fe. The morning after his family had spent the night, his mother took Carlos to an art gallery near their motel. He'd never been to an art gallery. Seeing the artwork on display and listening to his mother talk with the actual artist lit him up.

That afternoon, he mentioned the idea of enrolling in Santa Fe Community College and moving to Santa Fe to his mother. She was thrilled.

That evening, she mentioned it to her husband. A few minutes later, he stepped into the family room. Carlos was in the recliner, watching TV.

"Turn that off," his father said.

Carlos grabbed the remote and turned off the TV.

"What's up, Dad?"

"Mom told me you're thinking about going to art school."

"That's right. Santa Fe Community College."

"What's wrong with the University of New Mexico?"

"It's too expensive, and it's a four-year program. I could never afford it."

"You could get a loan."

"Yeah, but then I'd have huge debt when I got out, and I might never be able to pay it off."

"But UNM is a *real* college."

"Santa Fe Community College is a real college too."

"It's a trade school."

"It's what I need, Dad. It's what I want."

His father looked away.

"Te morirás de hambre," he said.

Carlos did the translation in his head. *You'll starve.*

"No, I won't, Dad. I'll be fine."

"I had such high hopes for you."

"What are you talking about?"

His father held out his hands, palms up.

"Look at my hands, Carlos. They're thick with callouses. My fingers have been broken. My hands hurt all the time. I've worked hard to give you a good start, not like the one I had, so that you could go to college and have a better life. And now you want to go to a trade school. You'll never make any money as an artist. You disappoint me, Carlos. You make me feel like a failure."

Carlos sat up. He felt angry. But he also felt sorry for his father. In that moment, he decided to put his anger aside.

"Dad, you've always worked so hard for us. And you know what? I've never said thank you. I want you to know how much I appreciate what you'd done for me. You *have* given me a better life. I'm going to college, and I'm going to be an artist. I'm going to be a good artist, and I know one day, you'll be proud of me."

His father had come into the room to object. He had a vision for his son, and he was there to try to force it on him one last time. But now he realized Carlos was his own man and that he needed to let him go to follow his own path.

With moist eyes, he looked at Carlos and said, "Will you do me a favor?"

"What's that?"

"Will you cut the grass tomorrow?"

Carlos was stunned by the question. But then he realized it wasn't really a question. It was a relinquishing. It was a sign of trust.

"Sure, Dad. I'd be happy to."

"Good. There's plenty of gas for the mower in the garage," he said, getting up.

"Thanks, Dad."

"Get some rest."

Then his father left and went upstairs.

Five years later, Carlos had his own art gallery in Taos. The grand opening was very well attended. Artists from Taos and Santa Fe were there. They were Carlos' colleagues and friends. Some were his students. Even the mayor and a local TV news crew showed up.

But to Carlos, the most important guests of all were his parents.

## A Final Message

I have a story I've never told anyone. I thought I'd take it to my grave, but dying changes the way you think.

In the time I have left, I'm going to write it down. Maybe it will do somebody some good.

It was June 1967, the Summer of Love. I'd just graduated from high school and started working at the root beer stand in town. I was making $1.40 an hour, enough to buy my books for college that fall with some beer money left over.

I worked mainly in the kitchen, but sometimes I worked out front, where we got to talk to the carhops.

Most of them were high school girls. One was older, though. Her name was Linda. She was 19. She'd gone to a different high school, and I didn't know her. But from the moment I first saw her, I was captivated.

Linda had long blond hair and big blue eyes. She laughed a lot. Her teeth were perfect. She was lean but filled out her white uniform in all the right places. She sashayed to waiting cars like a runway model.

I like to think I was attractive. In high school, I played football and ran track. I was in good shape. Regardless, Linda was out of my league. When she introduced herself and seemed interested in me, I was shocked.

"So I hear you're going to college," she said.

"Yeah. This fall. How about you?"

"No. I'll never go to college."

"Why not?"

"I'm not book smart."

"Oh."

"I'm smart in other ways, though," she said with a grin. Then she cat-walked away. Every time we saw each other the rest of that night, she grinned. It made me wonder what she meant about being smart in other ways.

Linda and I kept chatting at work. She asked where I lived, what I was going to study ... and how I got to work.

"I ride my bike," I said sheepishly.

"You don't drive?"

"I do, but I don't have a car."

"Really? I'd be happy to give you a ride sometime."

"Thanks, but I wouldn't want to put you out."

"You wouldn't be putting me out. If we're working the same shift, I'd be happy to give you a ride."

"Are you sure?"

"Uh huh. Do you work tomorrow?"

"Yeah. Noon to six."

"Me too. How about I pick you up about quarter til?"

I could hardly believe this was happening.

"Okay," I said.

I wrote my address on the back of an order slip and handed it to her. She folded it and slid it into her breast pocket. Patting her pocket, she smiled.

"See you tomorrow," she said.

The next day, Linda picked me up at the end of my driveway in a red VW Beetle. It smelled of cigarette smoke. The engine rumbled behind me. My seat vibrated. We were so cramped that our arms touched. Linda handled the stick shift with authority. That turned me on.

"So, do your parents expect you home right after work?" she said.

"I guess so."

"That's too bad."

"What do you mean?"

"Well, I thought you might want to grab a bite to eat."

"I'd like that. Maybe some other time."

"You're on," she said with a grin.

A few days later, Linda and I worked the same shift again, and Linda picked me up again. I told my mom I'd be going out with some friends after work.

After work, Linda took me back to her place, an apartment across town. She wanted to change before we went out.

"Make yourself at home," she said, locking her door behind me. "I'll be right back."

She slowly stepped across the main room and gently closed a door behind her. I assumed it was her bedroom.

I sat down in an armchair and looked around the small apartment. The white walls were bare, and there wasn't much furniture. I wondered if Linda had just moved in.

A few minutes later, the bedroom door opened, and out stepped Linda, wearing hip huggers and a pink halter top. My whole body felt warm.

She walked over and held out her hands. I got up and took them.

"Hungry?" she said.

"Yeah."

"What are you in the mood for?"

Before I could answer, Linda slid her hands behind my neck, pulled me close and kissed me hard.

We didn't make it to dinner that evening.

Before that summer, I'd never had sex. By the end of the summer, I "worked late" a lot.

And by the end of the summer, I'd fallen in love with Linda. I looked forward to being with her and not just for the sex. It was fun to be with her. We shared openly and easily. Our time together always seemed too short.

But as the summer drew to a close, Linda suddenly stopped offering to pick me up for work. I wanted to know why, but we really couldn't talk at work, so I called her at home.

"What's going on?" I said.

"What do you mean?"

"I mean you've stopped picking me up. I don't see you anymore."

"You need to get ready for college."

"Well, I've been thinking I might not go just yet."

"What?"

"I might take a year off before I start."

"Why would you do that?"

"To be with you."

There was a pause. Then Linda said, "Look, Jim, it's been fun, but you need to get on with your life."

"Is that what you want?"

"Yeah, it is. I need to get on with my life too, you know. I mean I can't work at the root beer stand forever."

I couldn't believe it. How could this woman I was in love with, and who I thought was in love with me, be saying this?

But I knew from Linda's tone something had changed. Her voice was no longer playful. She sounded anxious.

"Okay. I guess I'll leave for college. But can I see you again before I go?"

"I'm not sure that's a good idea. It would only make it harder."

But I did see Linda at work again. She smiled at me, but it wasn't the same. All summer, her smile had been like some special code between us. There was something in it just for me. Now she smiled at me like she smiled at everyone. It was then that I knew it was over.

About a week later, I left for college. My classes were okay, but I had a hard time concentrating. Linda was always on my mind.

I wrote her every few days, but I didn't hear back. Then one afternoon, I found an envelope under my dorm room door, with "Linda Harrison" printed in the upper left corner.

My heart beat fast and hard. I picked up the envelope, sat down on my bed and opened it.

Dear Jim,

Thanks for your letters. I'm sorry I haven't written, but this has been kind of a tough time for me.

I think I might be pregnant. But please don't worry. I don't blame you. It's my fault. I'll take care of everything.

I've decided to make some changes in my life. I'll be moving away soon, so there's no need to write me again. I hope you don't take that the wrong way. You're a great guy, and I enjoyed our time together this summer. I just need to make a fresh start.

Thanks for everything.

Linda


I couldn't believe what I was reading. Linda's pregnant? And I'm the father? And this is how she's telling me? What does she mean by "I'll take care of everything"? Is she going to have the baby or not? Don't I have a say in this?

I grabbed some change, ran down to the hall to a pay phone and dialed Linda's number.

"That'll be 50 cents for the first three minutes," the operator said.

I slipped in two quarters. I heard the operator dialing, then a ring. It rang and rang, but no one picked up. Maybe Linda's working, I thought. Or maybe she's already moved away.

Over the next couple of days, I tried to call Linda half a dozen more times, but there was still no answer. I wanted to talk to her so badly. I would have taken off for her apartment, three hours away, but I didn't have a car or know anybody who did.

I read Linda's letter over and over. I stared at one sentence in particular. *I think I might be pregnant.* What if she's not really pregnant? What if she's just saying that to cut me loose? How will I ever know the truth?

Not knowing for sure was driving me crazy. But what could I do? There was no way to reach Linda and no one to talk to about my situation. I felt so alone.

The whole thing was making me sick. I couldn't sleep. I skipped meals. I started drinking. I skipped classes. I dropped a class. My midterm grades were a disaster. My mom wrote me to make sure I was okay. I assured her I was. I hated lying to my mother.

I hitched a ride home for Thanksgiving. The first thing I did was drive over to Linda's apartment. But someone else was living there now.

I called Linda's parents' home. Her mom told me she had moved to Chicago.

I went to see a friend of Linda's named Peggy who had also been a carhop at the root beer stand. She'd worked with Linda the rest of that summer. I told Peggy I'd heard Linda might be pregnant.

"Well, if that's the case, she never mentioned it," Peggy said. "She sure wasn't showing."

This made me wonder if Linda really was pregnant. On my Christmas break, I called Linda's mom again. She told me Linda had a new job in Chicago — and a new boyfriend.

"I'm glad to hear she's doing well," I said.

"I think she's very happy."

It sure didn't sound like Linda was pregnant.

After that, I decided to move on with my life too. I returned to school and got serious about my studies. My midterm grades were excellent. My mom even wrote to congratulate me.

I started taking care of myself too. I ate well, stopped drinking and started running.

One day my roommate told me a girl named Kimberly in our economics class had asked about me.

"So?" I said.

"So? Man, she's a fox!"

"I'm not interested."

The truth was I felt so burned by my experience with Linda that I didn't want to risk getting into a relationship with anyone. In fact, I was growing suspicious of nearly everyone.

Intellectually, I knew I should be more trusting. But emotionally, my experience with Linda had made me gun-shy.

So I withdrew from the social scene and kept my interactions at school to a minimum. I had never been an extrovert, but now I was becoming a loner.

I graduated *magna cum laude* with a degree in finance. I got hired right away as an assistant manager by a bank in Indianapolis.

The job was okay. It wasn't very interesting, but I didn't have to deal with customers. I pretty much kept to myself. No lunches with co-workers or parties for me.

I was aware I was getting a reputation as an odd duck, but I didn't care. My experience with Linda was never far from my mind. I decided to never allow myself get too close to anyone again.

From time to time, I wondered if I was overreacting. I also wondered if Linda's decision to stop seeing me wasn't really about me at all, but about her and what she was going through at the time.

But I couldn't deny how what she did made me feel, and I couldn't risk getting hurt again. Better to be lonely than broken-hearted.

I worked at the bank for 35 years. After I retired, I started walking every day. I was feeling fine until about six months ago, when I felt a dull pain in my stomach. At first, the pain came and went, but then it was constant and got worse.

My doctor sent me to the hospital for tests. I found out I have stage four pancreatic cancer.

The doctors say it's not always fatal anymore and I could increase my chance of survival with chemotherapy or radiation. But there are no guarantees, and I don't trust doctors anyway, so I'm opting for palliative care when the time comes, probably very soon.

I wrecked my life. Not by having a fling with Linda that summer but allowing that experience to make everyone suspect.

I've lived in a prison of my own making. I've forfeited everything. Now I'll die unknown and unloved.

We all have experiences we regret. Don't let yours keep you from living your life. Whatever happens, be free.

# Bully

Some of Sam Logan's earliest memories were of being pushed around by bigger kids in his neighborhood. Nearly all the kids there were bigger than Sam. Some were pretty rough with him, but he never fought back. He was too afraid, and no one ever stood up for him. Even his older, and much bigger, brother never came to his defense.

"It'll toughen him up," he said.

But all the bullying didn't toughen Sam up. Instead, it made him feel insecure. It made him feel alone. It made him believe the world was out to get him.

In grade school, Sam was always the smallest boy in his class. But when he turned 14, he began to grow — and fast. By 16, he'd become one the biggest guys in his sophomore class.

The coaches at his high school tried to recruit Sam for their teams. But being so small and so easily intimidated as a kid, he hadn't played sports. He didn't know how to play football or basketball, and he wasn't about to make that obvious to his peers.

Then one day, his school's wrestling coach, Mr. Fenning, approached him.

"Have you ever considered wrestling, Sam? I think you could be great."

"I don't know. I've never wrestled."

"If you're willing to learn, I can teach you."

"I'll think about it."

That night, getting ready for bed, Sam checked out his impressive physique in his mirror. He'd been lifting his brother's weights in their basement for two years. Nobody's going to push me around anymore, he thought.

At school the following morning, before classes began, Sam walked into Fenning's homeroom and told him, "I'll do it."

Fenning first taught Sam the basics of wrestling: moves, terms and scoring rules. Then he had Sam practice with a couple of seniors. They both pinned him right away. But Sam learned fast, and within a few weeks, he was pinning them.

Sam wrestled with a vengeance, pinning every teammate he took on. It was as if he had found an outlet for all the frustration he had felt being bullied as a kid.

In his first match against another school, Sam pinned his opponent within the first two-minute period. He was thrilled, and his teammates' hearty congratulations bolstered his self-confidence.

In his next match, feeling emboldened, Sam picked up his opponent and slammed him down hard, a move he knew was illegal.

"Foul!" cried the ref.

But Sam didn't care, and he did it again. This time, the ref called the match. Sam had lost.

In the locker room, Fenning said, "Don't ever pull that stunt again."

"Okay," Sam said.

But in his next match, he did the same thing. The ref didn't call the match, but Sam lost on points.

"You're on the bench next week," Fenning told him afterwards.

Sam was so angry he quit on the spot.

At school, word got around about Sam body slamming wrestlers. Some began calling him a bully. Some students even started steering clear of him in the hallways.

Sam hadn't set out to become a bully. But after a lifetime of fearing others, he could get used to the idea of being feared.

Sam had become a handsome young man. As a freshman in college, he turned a lot of heads. However, the young women on campus soon learned what the girls in Sam's high school already knew: he was self-centered and demeaning.

Sam's first roommate came to the same conclusion and switched rooms after Christmas break. His second roommate didn't re-up. No one wanted to live with Sam. After his freshman year, he lived alone in a small apartment off-campus.

A Business 101 course was Sam's first glimpse into the world of business. It lit him up. He liked the idea of being the boss. He could see himself as a CEO one day.

In his sophomore year, Sam declared finance as his major. He studied hard, got great grades and did internships with five different companies. By the time he graduated, Sam had 10 offers.

He went with an energy company named ESG. It was large and global, with operations in both traditional and renewable energy. Most important to Sam, there was ample opportunity for promotion.

He started as an analyst. He was a quick study and a hard worker. Six months into the job, he'd been tagged by management as a "strong development candidate."

Sam got new assignments every 18 months, a clear sign he was being groomed. Within five years, he'd been promoted twice. Within

10, he was a vice president. By the time he was 35, Sam was leading one of ESG's four major business units, the youngest president in the company's history.

His business results were outstanding, but he'd gained a reputation as a very tough boss. At first, Sam treated his direct reports reasonably well. He knew he was being closely watched by management, so he made a conscious effort to be on his best behavior. But the higher he rose in the organization, the rougher he was on people.

This raised some eyebrows, but Sam had been tagged as a star. The only "discipline" he received was having to attend a training session on "managing inclusively."

"This will go in your file," his manager said with a wink.

Sam went on a lot of dates. But most women he went out with were turned off by his arrogance, so he had very few second dates.

One woman, though, a green-eyed beauty named Vanessa, kept seeing him. She pretended to be interested in Sam, but she cared much more about his bank account. When she hinted at marriage, Sam bought a ring with a huge diamond and proposed. Vanessa eagerly said yes.

Their marriage lasted six months. Vanessa sued for divorce and sought half of Sam's net worth. Sam hired a high-powered attorney, who got Vanessa to agree to a deal that would give her less money but allow her to keep their house and his Porsche Panamera.

For Sam, the whole experience revived his childhood feelings that the world was out to get him. To protect himself, he decided he would never date again.

Wounded and angry, Sam delved into his business with an even harder edge. He demanded a fresh review his entire business unit.

As a result, he recommended divesting several slower-growing, less profitable operations, investing more in certain renewable energies and acquiring a start-up that had invented a promising new battery technology.

The board had to approve all these moves. ESG's CEO, Brendan Quinn, decided to bundle them as one recommendation, which he asked Sam to present to the board.

Sam knew this was a unique career-enhancing opportunity. It was customary for company executives to bring at least a handful of technical experts to these board meetings to help answer questions. Sam showed up alone. He was intimately familiar with his proposed deals, and he handled every question with clarity and confidence. The board was impressed and approved all his recommendations.

Next Sam turned his attention to "right-sizing" his organization accordingly. He asked each of his direct reports for plans to cut headcount by 25%.

"These are pretty heavy cuts," Quinn said when Sam told him about his plan.

"We have far more people than we need," Sam said. "These cuts will greatly improve both our efficiency and our margins."

"I'm sure," Quinn said. "But have you thought about the impact on morale?"

"Yeah, I have. I think this move will toughen people up."

Under Sam's leadership, his business unit became the best-performing in the company. His employee attrition rate was also the highest in the company. But Sam worried about that only if it looked like his bottom line would be impacted. When that was the case, he hired new people fast and put even more pressure on his direct reports.

As Quinn neared retirement, Sam knew he was a long shot to succeed him, given he wasn't even 40. In fact, he wasn't Quinn's preferred successor. Quinn liked Sam's business results but felt he was a bully. Quinn has spent his entire career with ESG. He cared deeply about the company, and he wasn't about to turn it over to a bully.

But the board saw things differently. It had supported Quinn as CEO, but a number of board members felt he was "soft." The whole board had been impressed by Sam. They knew about the high attrition rate in his organization. But they were concerned ESG as a whole had grown fat and could some of the belt-tightening that Sam had done in his business unit.

Most important, the board felt Sam could take ESG to the next level. He had a killer instinct. As for his youth, they saw it as a plus.

"He'll be good PR for us," one board member said.

When the board chair told Quinn the board expected Sam to be ESG's next CEO, Quinn knew it was a done deal. He gave in and even announced Sam as his successor to the organization with a grace that belied his heavy heart.

For a while, Sam was indeed "good PR" for ESG. Being the youngest CEO in the energy industry, he attracted a lot of positive press.

But soon enough, Sam's penchant for efficiency and callous disregard for people led to major employee cuts across ESG. Investors loved it, and ESG's stock price soared. But employees panicked. Many left, including some of the company's most important players.

Sam seemed unconcerned. The board had told him they felt the company was "fat," and he knew the board had his back. In fact, the day the cuts were announced, the board chair had sent a bottle of Dom Perignon to Sam's office.

His employee cuts were just Sam's opening act as CEO. He quickly shifted gears to finding and securing new sources of growth for ESG.

His mergers and acquisitions (M&A) team had identified half a dozen attractive prospects.

Sam had dominated his employees. Now it was time to dominate his competitors. Sometimes, he thought about how he had felt as a boy, how timid and afraid he was of nearly everyone. He wished the neighbor kids could see him now. Little Sam Logan had grown up, and now he was not to be f***ed with. He was to be feared. Sam had picked his takeover targets, and he got ready to go after them.

He had his M&A team work up a deal sheet on each takeover target. Then, one by one, Sam himself called his counterpart at the other company. Sometimes the other CEO was cordial, and Sam knew they would be able to do business. But sometimes the other CEO was cagy or even hostile, and Sam knew he would have to play hard ball.

Either way, ESG prevailed. Sam set an aggressive goal of making two big plays a year. With Sam leading the way, ESG reached that goal three years in a row.

Sam promised investors that each of these acquisitions would be "accretive" in two years. In other words, the money ESG spent to buy a company would be made up by then.

Everyone knew there was only one way to accomplish that. ESG had to cut the number of people working for the companies it acquired. Eliminating some duplicative roles was to be expected, but Sam insisted on further job cuts. This made the newly acquired companies extremely light on people.

"It'll make us more agile," Sam said.

To some extent, he was right. But it also put enormous pressure on the organization to deliver on ESG's sales and profit projections. Sam knew his employees were burned out and that too many were leaving, but he didn't care. He simply told HR to ramp up recruiting.

One of ESG's potential acquisition targets was of particular interest to Sam. It was a small company, based in Brussels, which had developed a way to use hydrogen for fuel cells that are similar to batteries and can be used for powering an electric motor. Sam knew the company that could commercialize such a technology would make a fortune. He decided ESG must be that company.

As usual, he'd called the CEO, who said he was open to a deal "at the right price." Wasting no time, Sam left the following evening for Brussels on his company plane, a Gulfstream G650ER, with his small M&A team and top lawyer in tow.

They flew overnight. The flight attendant had just collected their breakfast trays, and they'd begun their descent toward the Brussels airport when suddenly the plane began to shake violently.

"Seatbelts on, everyone," the pilot called out from the open cockpit.

The shaking got worse, and the plane dropped precipitously.

"Emergency landing!" the pilot shouted.

All the overhead compartments opened, and oxygen masks plopped out.

"Put on your masks!" the flight attendant said.

The plane was rocking and lurching so badly that she couldn't remain standing. She sat down, fastened her seat belt and put on her oxygen mask.

Sam heard the landing gear go down. He looked around. Everyone had a look of terror in their eyes.

"Hold on, everyone," he said in a loud, steady voice masking his own fear. "We're going to make it."

Sam put on his oxygen mask too. It was morning, and he could see the Belgian countryside out his window — rolling hills, farmland, scattered buildings and trees. He hoped the pilot could find a flat place to land.

Then the twin engines went silent, and the jet began to nosedive. Now the only sound was of Sam's fellow passengers crying and praying, and the only thing Sam could think about was how poorly he'd treated these people and so many others. He was not a religious man, but he prayed God would forgive him.

Sam looked out and saw rows of soybeans just below. Maybe we can land in this field, he thought. But then he saw big trees just ahead. Then there was an awful crash, and Sam was knocked out.

He came to in a bed, unable to move. He opened his eyes and tried to look around. Everything was white. He wondered if he had died. Then he heard a beep near his head.

With great effort, Sam turned his head toward the sound. He saw medical devices and an IV and knew he was in a hospital. He remembered the plane going down. He remembered seeing soybeans and trees. But then, feeling groggy, he passed out.

He woke up the following day. He could hear someone in the room.

"Hello?" he said weakly.

He heard footsteps approaching his bed. Looking up, he saw a nurse. She smiled.

"You're awake, Mr. Logan," she said with a heavy accent.

"Where am I?"

"You're in a hospital in Brussels."

"What happened?"

"Your plane crashed. You're lucky to be alive."

"How are the others?"

Her face fell. She took his hand.

"I am very sorry to tell you there were no other survivors."

Sam gasped.

"What do you mean?"

"Your plane was completely disabled. Your pilot tried to land in a field but crashed into a woods. The rescue crew was shocked to find anyone alive. I'm very sorry for your great loss, Mr. Logan."

Sam closed his eyes and tried to comprehend what she had just told him. How could this have happened? He'd flown on that jet many times, without incident. And how could all the others be dead?

"How long have I been here?"

"Nearly a week."

"Their bodies were all flown back to the United States."

There were eight of us on that flight, Sam thought. Seven funerals. Seven families. He could hardly bear the thought.

"What is my condition?"

"You have many broken bones. Several of your internal organs were seriously injured. You were in surgery a long time. I'm not sure about the lasting effects. Now that you're awake, the doctor will give you a full report."

Later that day, Sam learned that three of his vertebrae had been fractured and his spinal cord had been damaged, though fortunately not severed. Only time would tell if he would be able to walk again.

Because of the extent of his injuries, his doctor advised Sam to undergo rehab at a nearby facility once he was released from the hospital. Flying back to the US at that point would be too risky.

Sam was also briefed on the crash. The initial report pointed to mechanical failure, metal fatigue brought on by the hull's pressurization cycle. Routine maintenance should have uncovered such a problem. But Sam had used his corporate jet so much lately that some safety checks had been skipped.

He learned the pilot, co-pilot, flight attendant and all five of the other passengers had been killed upon impact. Sam just happened to be in the only seat not destroyed.

And Sam learned his chief operating offer, Vanessa St. James, had been put in charge of ESG until he was ready to return.

The only two people who had reached out to him were St. James and Max Ledger, chairman of ESG's board.

Ledger had sent a brief telegram to let Sam know the board was putting St. James in charge temporarily. He'd also sent a bouquet of flowers on behalf of the board.

St. James had sent a much longer telegram.

Dear Sam,

I was so sorry to learn of your accident.

I am grateful that you survived though deeply saddened by the loss of our colleagues, the pilot and crew. I will represent us at their funerals.

I will do my best to guide ESG in your absence, following through on your plans. I will arrange for a Zoom call so we can talk when you are feeling up to it.

In the meantime, if you need me for anything, please let me know.

I am praying for your fast and full recovery. Take good care.

Vanessa

To Sam, Ledger sending flowers was surprising because it seemed so soft. He assumed Ledger's secretary had actually done it.

Vanessa's note, though, was not surprising. It reflected the thoughtfulness and empathy he had come to expect from her.

She was the president of one of ESG's four major businesses, the only woman at that level. Sam had promoted her several years earlier, not because he wanted to but because the board was putting pressure on him to improve diversity.

But Sam had been pleasantly surprised by both Vanessa's impressive business results and her positive impact on her organization.

She seemed to genuinely care about her people. She invested as much time in her organization as she did her business, and employee turnover on her business was far lower than that of any other ESG business. In fact, some on other businesses requested transfers to hers.

Sam would not have admitted it, but deep down he knew Vanessa's strong business results were due in part to how well she managed people. He suspected Ledger knew this too.

All of it gave Sam pause. For the first time, with the exception of his moment of regret as his plane was going down, he reflected on his life.

For decades, he had treated people harshly, as he had been treated as a child. He was a bully. He had no friends or family. His parents were gone, and he was long estranged from his brother.

Now, 6,000 miles from home, disconnected from his company, which had become his life, he felt alone and insecure, just as he had as a boy.

Over the course of weeks, it became clear that Sam would walk again. His injuries had begun to heal, but his full recovery was going to take time and now require physical therapists and other specialists. His doctor decided it was time for Sam to move to rehab, and he was transported to a nearby facility.

The first person Sam met there was a woman named Bernadette Jacobs. She would be him primary aide. She was middle-aged and pretty, petite with auburn hair and an easy smile. She spoke with a heavy accent, but her English was perfect. She seemed refined. Sam wondered what she was doing working there.

"May I call you Sam?" she said straight away.

After a moment's pause, Sam said, "Yes."

He was used to being called Mr. Logan. Everyone at the hospital had called him that.

But he quickly learned Bernadette was not like the others. She too was a top-notch health care professional, but she was also warm and seemed to genuinely care about Sam, not just as a patient but as a person.

And she was kind to him. Not that the hospital personnel had been unkind. But they all knew Sam was the CEO of a major company. They were deferential and always professional. But they'd never gone beyond their clinical duties. No one there had ever even asked Sam about his life.

After establishing she could call him Sam, Bernadette next asked Sam where he was from. It was a simple question, but no one at the hospital had posed it. Sam told Bernadette he was from a small in Upstate New York. She hadn't been to the US, and she asked him about his childhood home and what his childhood was like.

Sam had never told anyone the truth about his childhood because the truth was too hard and too embarrassing for him to express. But here was a person who seemed to really want to know, who did not seem in any way out to get Sam and who he knew he would likely soon never see again.

And so he told her the truth. He told her about being bullied and how this made him feel. He told her about his brief time as a wrestler in high school and how that experience had changed him, how he had become a bully.

As he shared this, Sam began to cry. He hadn't shed a tear in years. Now here he was, weeping in front of a relative stranger. He wondered what she would think of him. He felt so vulnerable. Had he said too much?

Her reaction surprised him. She handed him a tissue and simply said, "If you are comfortable, Sam, please tell me more."

In the coming days and weeks, Sam told Bernadette everything. He told her about his college years, about his short-lived marriage, about his career. He even told her about the plane crash and how he felt responsible.

"Did you know those people well?" she said.

"I wasn't close to any of them, but I knew them all, especially my employees."

"Have you reached out to their families?"

"No."

"If I got you some stationery, would you like to write them letters?"

Sam hadn't considered reaching out to the families of those who had lost their lives in the crash. For a moment, he wondered if doing so might be tantamount to admitting guilt for their deaths. But he put that concern aside and said, "Yes."

He wrote eight letters, apologizing for his delay, explaining he had just begun rehab. By then, he was in regular email contact with Vanessa. Her office gave Sam the names of next of kin and their addresses.

The act of writing these letters began to change Sam. To express his condolences, to tell the loved ones of his former colleagues and the crew how much he valued them, to articulate their best traits took Sam far beyond his comfort zone. For the first time in his adult life, he felt not like a detached businessman or a bully but a human being.

And the process of writing eight letters helped him to realize how fortunate he was to have survived the crash. He felt guilty that he alone had been spared. He wondered why he too had not perished.

He was shocked when all the people he wrote sent him notes in return to thank him and wish him a speedy recovery. He thought they might blame him. Instead, most told him he was in their prayers. Every note made him wish he had thanked his employees for all they had done for ESG.

Sam spent three months in rehab, and Bernadette was with him nearly every day. Being near her changed him. No one had been kind to him in a very long time, and her kindness began to open his heart. It made him think about the kind of person he really wanted to be.

And his regular Zoom calls with Vanessa made him think differently about his job. Vanessa was running ESG very effectively and with an advocacy for people that Sam had never shown. There is no reason she should not be CEO when I'm healthy enough to return, he thought.

But what would that mean for him? Although he had cared little for the people of ESG, he cared deeply about the company itself. It was the only place he had ever worked.

Sometimes, Bernadette would push Sam around the rehab center in a wheelchair. He was amazed by how pristine Brussels was. He had known Europe was far ahead of the US when it came to renewable energy. But now he could see the benefits for himself, and it made him realize ESG had an opportunity to help lead the US and the world in the right direction when it came to the environment.

Would he need to continue as CEO in order for ESG to play such a role? No. With a capable CEO like Vanessa at the helm, Sam knew he could play an important and helpful role as chairman. I'll talk with Ledger, he thought.

In the meantime, Sam continued to heal. He had been brought to Brussels in an ambulance, a broken man and a bully. Five months later, he left transformed by kindness.

## Bare Essence

Success always comes with enemies. During the last half of the twentieth century, Joe Dawson became one of the most successful men in Newark, Ohio. He did this despite all the obstacles thrown in his way by another successful man in Newark named Mike Wolf.

Dawson and Wolf grew up 30 miles apart. Their paths first crossed when they were both 21. Dawson was just starting to build houses in Newark, and Wolf had just been elected the city's youngest-ever councilman.

Each was following in the footsteps of his father. Dawson's father worked in a factory and built one or two houses a year as a way to supplement his income. Wolf's father was Newark's city clerk.

During their summers as teenagers, Dawson helped his father build houses, and Wolf sometimes tagged along with his father at city hall. Their fathers had something in common. They understood where the power was in the kind of work they did, and they knew they didn't have it.

Dawson's father taught him how to build a house. He also taught him the only way to make any real money in that business was to develop land and build a lot of houses.

Wolf's father taught him about issuing construction permits. He also taught him the real power lay in zoning land and determining who built what where.

But whereas Dawson's father respected developers and home builders, Wolf's father viewed them with contempt.

"They rape the land," the elder Wolf told his son.

The early 1950s were a boom time in America. In Ohio, Columbus was expanding in all directions, and the residents of traditional coal mining towns were moving west for better jobs. Newark was right in the middle. A number of companies opened or expanded facilities there, and people started moving in.

Dawson and Wolf had just finished tours of duty in Korea. Dawson served in the Air Force, Wolf in the Navy. Both were ambitious and too eager to get to work to bother with college.

Building houses was in Dawson's blood, and he had paid attention to his father's advice. He wanted to build a lot of houses and develop land too.

Although he considered his father's job boring, Mike Wolf had developed a keen interest in the workings of city hall. In the Navy, he was surprised when some of his fellow sailors looked to him for direction. He realized he had leadership potential. When he returned home, he decided to run for an open city council position. That November, he won.

Dawson wanted to buy some old farmland near an industrial park. He thought it would be a good place for a new subdivision. He approached the farmer, who was happy to sell his property and gave him a good price.

Dawson asked his father for a loan. He was glad to loan his son money, but it couldn't loan him enough to cover the cost of the property. So he asked a handful of his friends if they would make small loans too. Several said yes.

Dawson was thrilled. He now had enough to buy the land and begin developing it. However, it would need to be rezoned from agricultural to residential. His father told him he would need to submit a proposal to the city's planning commission.

To help him do that, Dawson had to hire a local attorney. He didn't like spending any of his precious loan money this way but had no other option.

A few months later, his proposal had been submitted and was scheduled for a hearing before the planning commission. These hearings were held in the evening. Dawson attended, and his father came with him.

Planning commission meetings in Newark were usually brief. The five commission members were supportive of growth in the city, and proposals were nearly always approved.

As a new councilman, Wolf had begun attending planning commission meetings, even though he wasn't a member. He said it was to get up-to-speed on development in the city.

Wolf too had listened to his father. Even though he had no experience dealing with developers and builders, he remembered what his father had told him about them.

Wolf also knew that developers up to that point had largely been given carte blanche in Newark. He knew he couldn't stop the city from growing, but he also knew he now had a hand in regulating that growth.

In his proposal, Dawson had stated the price range he envisioned for the houses that would be built on his land. They would be more expensive than most homes in Newark. Wolf's father had never made much money, and Mike had a bias against the rich. He was concerned that Dawson's new homes might set a precedent and ultimately make Newark less affordable for people like his parents.

Once Dawson's proposal was read aloud, there was an opportunity for questions before commission members voted on it. Wolf raised his hand and stepped over to a microphone in the center aisle.

"Michael Wolf," he said.

"Yes, Mr. Wolf," said Stuart Rice, the commission chair. "We know who you are."

Everyone laughed.

"Mr. Chairman, that tract of land sits low, doesn't it?"

Rice seemed taken aback by the question. He looked at the other members, who shrugged or shook their heads.

"I'm not sure, Mr. Wolf. Do you have a concern about the elevation?"

"Yes, I'm concerned about flooding."

"Flooding?"

"Yes, I'm concerned that land might be sitting in a flood plain."

"A flood plain? Mr. Wolf, it's farmland."

"It used to be farmland, but it hasn't been used for that purpose for years, and that new industrial park nearby has created a lot of runoff."

Rice looked annoyed.

"Do you have a specific suggestion or request, Mr. Wolf?" he said.

"Yes, I think the area should be surveyed to make sure it's suitable for building houses, possibly a lot of houses."

Rice turned to the man to his left.

"Has that area been surveyed lately, Len?"

"No. The last survey was 20 years ago."

Rice looked at Dawson, as if he were hoping he might be able to speak to the issue. But neither Dawson nor his father knew what to say.

Looking back at Wolf, Rice said, "All right, Mr. Wolf, we'll look into it. In the meantime, we'll table this proposal pending reassurance from a new survey."

"Thank you, Mr. Chairman," Wolf said.

Heading back to his seat, Wolf looked over at the Dawsons with a kind of smirk on his face.

This was the first of many obstacles Wolf would throw in Dawson's way in the years to come. He did this for eight years as a city councilman in Newark, then 30 years as a commissioner for Licking County, named after the river that ran through it.

But Dawson was determined to become a successful developer and builder. Wolf tried hard to slow him down, but eventually Dawson always found ways around his challenges.

Ultimately, of course, Newark grew, despite Wolf's heavy hand, and Dawson became the city's leading developer and home builder. By the 1980s, nearly one in every two newer homes, apartments and condos in Newark had been built by Dawson.

Dawson was satisfied with his success, but Wolf was always after even more power. During his decades as county commissioner, he ran for state representative, US representative and governor. He lost every statewide race.

Dawson had a reputation as a fair and gracious businessman. Wolf had a reputation as a tough politician. Despite his losses at the state level, many of the people of Newark and Licking County saw Wolf as their advocate. He was a popular, high-profile local figure.

There was no love lost between the two men. Personally, Dawson thought Wolf was mean-spirited and considered him his only real enemy. Beyond his wife Betsy, though, Dawson never said a negative thing about Wolf.

By contrast, Wolf spoke ill of Dawson to anyone who would listen. To Wolf, Dawson was a poster boy for "growth at any price" in Newark.

Yet over the years, despite all the public meetings and events they both attended, the two men somehow never met.

By 1990, their long careers were winding down.

In many ways, the two men faced very different situations. For starters, Dawson had taken good care of himself over the years, and he was in good health. And he had made a small fortune.

Wolf had overindulged in food and drink, smoked and never exercised. By the time he retired, he had suffered a heart attack and was obese. He walked with a cane. Like his father, he'd never made much money. Now his main source of income was Social Security.

But the two men had something in common too. They had both lost their wives. Breast cancer had taken Betsy when she was 52. Barbara Wolf had been killed in a car accident when she was 54.

The Dawsons had no children. Soon after they were married, Betsy had several miscarriages. The young couple was devastated. They talked about adopting a child, but their lives got busy and, over time, the idea just seemed to slip away.

The Wolfs had one child, a daughter named Susan. She had Down syndrome. In the 1950s, many children born with this condition were taken away from their parents and "institutionalized." But Barbara insisted Susan be raised at home.

Wolf's busy work life meant Susan was, for the most part, raised by Barbara. Raising a child with such special needs was hard, but Barbara did it with love and grace. Wolf marveled at his wife. When she was killed, Susan was 29 and still living at home. Wolf was lost and unsure how to care for his daughter. Fortunately, a woman from the county's board of developmental disabilities reached out to him and helped arrange for in-home care.

At that point, for the first time in his career, Wolf got home in time for dinner every night. He tapped others to represent him at county meetings in the evenings. If he had to attend events on the weekends, he brought Susan with him.

Wolf had always loved his daughter but realized only then how little time he'd actually spent with her over the years. Now, he felt grateful to have this time with Susan.

And the experience of being there for her began to soften him.

In 2011, Dawson and Wolf both turned 80. By then, they'd both long been retired. Dawson still walked or biked several times a week, but Wolf was in terrible shape. He had suffered another heart attack and been diagnosed with emphysema. His mobility was quite limited, and now Susan was helping him.

One day, Dawson was riding his bike across an intersection. He had the right-of-way, but a car turned right, ran into him and knocked him over. He went down hard, and his left shoulder, left arm and left hip were broken. If he hadn't been wearing a helmet, he might have been killed.

After a two-week stay in the hospital, Dawson was moved to a rehab center. The idea was to spend a few weeks there. Once he was stable, he could receive care at home.

One morning, eating breakfast in bed, Dawson heard an aide across the hall say, "Will there be anything else, Mr. Wolf?"

He perked up and listened.

"No, thank you," a man said softly.

He knew that voice. When his aide came to take away his breakfast tray, Dawson asked if the man across the hall was Mike Wolf.

"Yes," she said. "He just got here yesterday."

Dawson couldn't believe it. He wondered what Wolf was doing there. Should he reach out to him? *Surely Wolf has no beef with me anymore*, he thought.

He paged his aide and asked her to ask Wolf if he would be open to having a visitor — specifically, one named Joe Dawson.

A few minutes later, she came back.

"He said yes."

Dawson asked her to wheel him across the hall to Wolf's room. When they got to the open door, Dawson knocked on the frame.

"Hello, Mike. May I come in?"

Wolf was in bed. He looked over at Dawson and said, "Yeah."

The room was small. The aide wheeled Dawson in and parked him near the window, facing Wolf.

"I'll let you two visit for a while," she said.

The two men sat staring at each other, saying nothing, for a long minute.

Then Dawson said, "How are you, Mike?"

Wolf was sitting up in bed. A plastic tube tucked behind his ears ran below his nose with two prongs fitting into his nostrils. His breathing was labored. He was pale and looked uncomfortable.

"Well, I'm in pretty bad shape, as you can see. I have emphysema. My doctor thinks the next step for me might be hospice. I doubt I'll be around much longer. What about you?"

"I'm sorry, Mike. I was riding my bike, and a car ran into me. A few broken bones. That's all. I'll heal."

"Aren't you a little old to be riding a bike?" Wolf said with a small smile.

It occurred to Dawson he had seldom seen Wolf smile.

"Maybe so," he said, smiling back.

The two men continued talking as if they were old friends, not longtime enemies. They didn't talk about their work. They talked about their time in Korea and their wives, and Wolf talked about Susan. Dawson had no idea Wolf had a daughter.

"I'm so worried about her," he said. "I don't know what will happen to her if I don't make it."

"Who's taking care of her now?"

"I've hired someone to come in once a day to check on her and bring her groceries. But if I die, I don't know who's going to look after her. There won't be much money left. Susan would be on her own."

"Do you have a family member who could take care of her?"

"No."

Dawson thought for a moment.

"Mike, do you have a will?"

"No, I don't," Wolf said, looking embarrassed.

"What if I asked my lawyer to come here and draw up a will for you? You could specify who would care for your daughter, you know, if something were to happen to you."

Wolf stared at Dawson.

"Joe, I gave you nothing but trouble for years. Why would you do something like that for me?"

"We were just doing our jobs, Mike. But those days are over. We're here now. Your daughter is going to need someone to care for her. I have a lawyer on retainer. He's not doing anything else for me right now. He could come over, spend an hour with you and prepare a will in a few days. No big deal."

"Well, it may not be a big deal to you, but it would mean a lot to me. If you're serious, yes, I'll take you up on your offer."

"I am serious. I'll call my lawyer today. He can come over whenever it's convenient for you."

"Well, my calendar's not very full these days," Wolf said with a chuckle that made him cough hard.

"You okay?"

"Yeah," Wolf said, closing his eyes and drawing a breath.

"Okay, then. I'll call him today."

"Thank you."

"Well, I'd better let you get some rest."

"Okay. It's been nice talking with you. Thanks again."

"Sure. If you need me, I'll be right across the hall."

The following morning, after breakfast, Dawson again asked his aide to ask Wolf if he was up for some company.

She checked.

"He said yes."

She wheeled him over to Wolf's room.

"How are you doing this morning?" Dawson said.

"About the same."

"Mike, I've been thinking. I have an idea I'd like to share."

"Sure."

"What if I become Susan's guardian?"

Wolf looked at Dawson as if he expected him to say something else.

"What?"

"I mean I have plenty of money, and I'm in good health. I could give Susan a good home. I mean, should something happen to you."

Wolf's eyes welled with tears.

"Why?" he said softly. "Why would you do this?"

"Betsy and I tried to have children for years. We prayed to have children. I've been successful in business, but there's been a big gap in my life. I'm not Susan's father, of course. But I know how important she is to you, and it would mean a lot to me to be able to care for her, just as you have."

Wolf closed his eyes, covered his face with his hands and began sobbing.

"It's okay," Dawson said. "It's okay."

Finally, Wolf stopped crying and wiped away his tears.

"Thank you," he said. "I would be honored to have you be my daughter's guardian."

The following day, Dawson's lawyer came by to meet with Wolf. Two days later, he came back with a will, which he, Wolf and Dawson signed. Two aides served as witnesses and signed it too.

Wolf arranged to have Susan brought to the rehab center so he could see her and she could meet Dawson.

"Susan, this is my friend. His name is Joe Dawson. He is going to look after you when Daddy has to go away. You'll live with him. He is a very nice man, and he has a beautiful house, and you'll like living with him very much."

"Okay, Daddy," she said with a smile.

As Wolf's condition grew worse, he slept more and more. As his own condition improved, Dawson would sometimes wheel himself over to Wolf's room while he was sleeping and just sit there, watching over him.

Sometimes he would think about all the years they were at odds and how it took ill health to bring them together and strip them to their bare essence and allow each of them to become an answer to the other's prayers.

# Calling

Bill Frazier was always drawn to news. By the time he was eight, he was reading his parents' newspaper, the *World-Herald*, all the way through. It was the first thing he did when he got home from school. He loved learning about what was happening in Omaha and beyond.

In those days, severe drought and massive dust storms were devastating much of the Great Plains. Bill read the accounts of these natural disasters and the human hardships they caused.

He also read stories that quoted experts on the need for soil conservation. He read editorials calling for legislation to protect the land. He read about Congress creating the Soil Conservation Service.

Bill began to realize the power of newspapers, not just in relaying information, but in shaping opinions and affecting change, and he felt something stir in his heart.

As a freshman at Central High, Bill started writing for the school paper, *The Register*. He learned how to gather news and develop stories. He learned how to interview people. He learned what it takes to put a newspaper together. He loved every bit of it.

In his sophomore year, Bill began writing editorials. At first, he wrote about issues at school, but those topics bored him. Bill was interested in the larger issues of the day, and he was surprised that many of his classmates didn't seem to know much about them.

He had read in the *World-Herald*, for example, about the dramatic changes taking place in Germany. He read about the rise of the Nazi party, its crackdown on Jews and a new law that allowed for the forced sterilization of Germans with "genetic disorders" — from schizophrenia to blindness.

When he read about these things, Bill was outraged. There was nothing he could *do* about them, of course, but he wanted the students in his school to *know* about them. He wanted them to know the truth. He didn't know how many of them read the *World-Herald*. But he knew a good number read *The Register*.

So he wrote an editorial entitled "Why Should We Care About What's Going on in Germany?"

*Germany may seem distant and not very relevant to our everyday lives. But it's not so far away. We trade with Germany. Ford, Coca-Cola and Kodak own and operate plants there. The United States has an embassy in Berlin. Many of our ancestors came here from Germany. Some of our relatives still live there.*

*What happens when such a country decides to no longer abide by its peace treaties, when it "appoints" a dictator to replace its elected leader, when it begins taking away civil liberties, when it blames Jews for its problems, when it rounds up and arrests its political opponents, when it burns books, when it sterilizes its "imperfect" citizens?*

*We Americans care deeply about freedom. So how can we do business as usual with a country where freedom is under attack? How can we look the other way when those now in power persecute their fellow countrymen because they bear the "wrong" birthmark? How long can we, the leading light of freedom in the world, sit idly by and not take a stand?*

*The Register* was published on Tuesdays. Copies were available to students on racks throughout the school. Usually, old copies from the previous week had to be removed when a new edition was published. But that Tuesday, every copy was gone by the time school was out.

Everyone read Bill's editorial. Students began talking about what was going on in Germany. Some wrote letters to the editor of *The Register* and even the *World-Herald*. The debate club took up the topic. The civics club wrote Nebraska's Congressmen, urging them to make a statement against the infringement of human rights in Germany. The valedictorian of the class of 1934 spoke about how events unfolding in Germany represented a threat to freedom everywhere.

The whole experience lit Bill up. He knew he'd done something important. That's when he felt called to become a journalist.

Six years later, Bill graduated from the University of Nebraska, where he majored in journalism and was editor of the student newspaper. Just before he graduated, he got an interview with Warren Margolis, the editor of the *World-Herald*. Margolis was so impressed that he offered Bill a job on the spot, even though he didn't have an open position.

"You might be a copyboy for a while," Margolis said.

"Sounds good to me," Bill said.

During his first year at the paper, "copyboy" turned out to be a pretty good job description for Bill. He edited reporters' copy. He did research for them. He even fetched their coffee.

But Bill didn't mind. He was working for a big-time newspaper, learning the ropes. What he didn't know is how he was impressing the reporters there. He made their stories better, and they talked him up with their editors.

"That boy can write," one said.

When the United States entered the Second World War, Omaha immediately began sending its sons abroad, and the people of Omaha were eager for news about the war. The editorial board of the *World-Herald* met to discuss how they would cover the conflict.

Of course, the *World-Herald* ran wire stories like every major newspaper in the country. But the editorial board decided to supplement this coverage with its own dispatches. The editors decided to assign one of their own reporters to cover the action.

When they thought about who could do the job, Bill's name came up. Though he was young, the editors knew Bill could write well and that he stayed on top of world affairs. Also, Bill still didn't have a regular beat at the paper. All in all, the editors thought Bill would be a great fit.

So they decided to offer him the assignment. When Warren Margolis approached him with the idea, Bill was thrilled. He knew the war was the biggest story in the world. The opportunity to see it up close and file dispatches to keep his fellow Nebraskans informed once again made Bill feel like he was being called.

In early 1942, Bill left for France, where he was embedded with an Army infantry unit. The plan was that he would stay at least six months. More than two years later, Bill was still in France. He had traveled all over Europe, staying close to the action and sending reports home in a column called "Up Close."

In June of 1944, Bill was part of the landing at Omaha Beach. He was unarmed, but in the madness, he was shot at, though thankfully not hit.

Bill spent nearly a week at Normandy, filing several dispatches a day. Readers in Nebraska were riveted. Everyone knew this was a turning point in the war. Everyone hoped the end was near.

Unfortunately, the war in Europe would rage on nearly another full year. Bill stayed to cover it. When Germany finally surrendered, Bill was in Berlin to report on the Allied victory.

"Freedom has triumphed," he wrote, in one of his last dispatches from Europe.

No sooner had Bill returned home when Warren Margolis asked him if he would be open to going to the Pacific and covering the action there.

"This will be the final chapter in the war," he said. "It's going to be brutal. I know what you've been through, and if you've had enough, I'll certainly understand. But people here hang on your every word. They trust you ..."

"Yes," Bill said, interrupting. "I'll do it."

Bill was on the island of Saipan, getting ready to cover the US invasion of the Japanese home islands, when the first atomic bombs were dropped.

Less than a month later, Bill was on the USS Missouri to cover the formal surrender.

"Today, on the deck of this battleship," he wrote, "I witnessed a new birth of freedom."

Bill returned to Omaha a kind of hero. To everyone there, he'd become a most trusted source of news about the war. Friends, neighbors and even strangers welcomed him home warmly. Most of them hadn't seen him in nearly four years. He'd become a man of the world — and a handsome young man.

One morning, grabbing coffee at a shop down the street from the *World-Herald*, Bill bumped into a former classmate at Central High, Marie Garnier. She was working there. Bill and Marie hadn't seen each other since high school.

She had blossomed into a beautiful woman. With her blue eyes, black hair and soft facial features, Marie reminded Bill of the lovely young women he'd seen in France. Until then, he hadn't really thought about her name.

"Is Garnier French?" he asked.

"Yes," she said. "My parents were born in France."

"*Je savais par ta beauté.*"

Marie blushed and smiled, and Bill saw something beyond beauty in her eyes.

He asked her to dinner. They fell in love. Six months later, they were married.

In the meantime, the *World-Herald* made Bill its city editor. At 28, he was the youngest editor in the newspaper's history.

But as accomplished as Bill was as a reporter, he found the transition challenging. Not because of his new editorial responsibilities, but because his world had suddenly shrunk and grown tame.

Bill was used to observing life and death drama in the fields, forests and jungles of faraway lands. Now his biggest challenge was navigating traffic in downtown Omaha.

It wasn't just the physical differences, though. Bill was struggling to make sense of the everyday practices he saw in Omaha that seemed at odds with what he had seen American soldiers fighting and dying for overseas.

He saw "separate but equal" facilities for Blacks. He saw books like *For Whom the Bell Tolls* and *The Grapes of Wrath* banned by the school board. He saw restrictive hiring practices by local businesses.

None of these things was new in Omaha. But Bill's experiences had given him new eyes. He now viewed things through the lens of the basic freedoms that had been under attack. What he had once considered normal, he now felt was wrong. As an editor for the most influential medium in the region, he now had a chance to expose common practices in his community that he now considered unfair and unjust.

And so under Bill's leadership, the city desk began running hard-hitting stories. Bill also wrote editorials. The *World-Herald* took heat from some community leaders, but Warren Margolis was a brave man who knew good journalism, and he always had Bill's back.

By 1952, Margolis was ready to retire. He recommended to his publisher that Bill succeed him. By then, Bill had distinguished himself as an award-winning journalist and editor. He'd even been nominated for a Pulitzer Prize for his editorials denouncing Senator Joseph McCarthy's campaign against alleged Communists in the US as anti-American.

Margolis' publisher readily agreed with his recommendation, and Bill soon took over as editor of the newspaper he'd begun reading as a boy.

By then, Bill and Marie had started a family. Bill loved being a father. He often thought of all the young men he had seen overseas who would never know the joy of becoming a father.

With Bill now at the helm of the *World-Herald*, the paper took a sharp left turn, championing social causes such as civil rights and even questioning America's involvement in Korea.

Many in Omaha appreciated the paper's more progressive approach. Some, though, took umbrage. Local business leaders and government officials demanded to meet with the editorial board. Bill and his editors listened to their concerns, but there was no let-up in what they saw as their professional responsibility.

Bill wasn't put off by the flak. He'd seen much worse, and he knew he was doing the right thing.

"People here can disagree," he said. "That's vital in a democracy."

Not all of Bill's critics, though, were civil. Some wrote letters to the editor, calling Bill a Communist, a socialist or worse. Many letters were filled with vulgarities.

Bill also got personal letters, including death threats. He turned those over to the police.

Marie was beside herself. Bill tried to reassure her he would be okay, that critics come with the territory.

"They're idle threats," he said. "They're just trying to back me off."

This only made Marie more anxious because she knew her husband would not back off.

One gray November evening, after Bill had parked his car in his garage, he walked down his driveway to his mailbox, as he did when he got home from work.

A pickup truck came down the street and rolled to a stop behind him. Just as he was reaching in to get his mail, someone reached through the open window and shot Bill in the back of the head.

The shocking murder was front-page news across the country. Condolences and tributes poured in from journalists around the world. The Sunday edition of the *World-Herald* featured a special section devoted to remembrances of Bill and his work. In Sunday services across the country, clergymen praised Bill as "an apostle for the truth."

Warren Margolis sounded that theme in his eulogy.

"Bill Frazier had a calling," he said. "It was to reveal the truth. He was struck down by an enemy of the truth, but the truth lives on. It is and always will be our guiding light, just as Bill was and always will be our inspiration."

The Army posted a color guard at the burial. The soldiers there carried rifles. They would have given Bill a three-volley salute, but they didn't fire their guns out of respect for Marie.

That summer, Central High was renamed William Frazier High School, and a journalism scholarship was established in Bill's honor. The University of Nebraska named its college of journalism for Bill. And Bill was posthumously awarded the Pulitzer Prize for local reporting.

But what would have been most meaningful to Bill happened quietly, if gradually, in Omaha. "Separate but equal" signs were removed. Public schools were integrated. Local companies began hiring more women and minorities.

It was the kind of positive change Bill had hoped could happen if people only understood, the kind of change he believed he could help bring about if he stayed true to his calling.

## The Adoption

In July 2020, under a blistering Afghan sun, near the border of Pakistan, 22-year-old Ben Germain leaned against a stone wall and waited for his captain's command. His company had surrounded a village where a group of Taliban fighters were holed up.

Ben was drenched with sweat and breathing hard. He wasn't sure what they were up against, but he was determined to do whatever was needed to take out these terrorists.

"Go!" his captain yelled.

Ben took a deep breath, pivoted from behind the wall and ran toward a house, less than 100 yards away. Someone was shooting through a window. Ben had to take the shooter out.

He ran as fast and low as he could. Bullets zinged by, but he reached the house unscathed. He was now near the open window, with his back pressed against the wall of the house. Someone was still firing from inside.

Ben slowly pulled a grenade from his belt, pulled the pin and lobbed the grenade through the window. He heard a man yell something in Pashto. Then there was a loud explosion. He felt the house rock and saw debris fly through the window. Then silence.

I got him, Ben thought.

But then he heard a woman screaming from inside. Was it a decoy? The Taliban were known to use civilians as human shields. The shooting had stopped, but Ben knew the enemy could still be lying in wait.

Slowly, he made his way to the door. He was ready to break it down but thought he would see if it was unlocked. He pushed on the wooden handle, and the door creaked open.

Inside, the screaming had turned to wailing. Ben listened carefully for the sound of a man or men but heard nothing but the wailing. He peeked inside and saw a man's bloody body sprawled on the floor. The air was thick with dust and the smell of metal.

The wailing was coming from the next room, whose wall had been partly blown away. Ben stepped carefully through the front room, around the man's lifeless body, toward the sound of the woman's voice.

He peeked around the doorway, his rifle at the ready. Inside the room, a small kitchen, a young woman knelt on the floor. She was covered with dust, and blood streamed down her face. She was holding something in her arms. At first, Ben wasn't sure what it was. Then, seeing him in the doorway, the woman screamed something and held up the bloody, lifeless body of a little girl, as if to show Ben what he had done.

Horrified, Ben froze. Then he heard his captain call, "They're in the mosque! Surround it! Now!"

The woman's wailing had now turned to moaning, as she cradled her dead daughter. It was the most awful thing Ben had ever seen. He wanted to stay and help. He wanted to tell the woman he was sorry, but he had to go.

Ben completed his tour in Afghanistan, but he didn't raise a weapon against another human being again. Once the captain got on him for hanging back. But between enemy attacks and casualties among his men, he had his hands full. After that, he let Ben be.

Ben knew that by not firing on the enemy, he could be putting his fellow soldiers at risk. He loved them like brothers, and he would always be at their side. But he simply couldn't kill again.

No one asked Ben why he stopped shooting. If they had, he couldn't have told them. The wound was too deep.

Soon after he returned home, Ben was honorably discharged from the Army. He did an exit interview, in part to determine what help he might need moving forward. He didn't mention what happened in that house in Afghanistan, and he said he was fine.

Back in his hometown of Davenport, Iowa, Ben got an apartment and a job as an Amazon driver.

That August, he watched TV coverage of the disastrous US withdrawal from Afghanistan in disbelief. He wondered if his service had been in vain.

Ben focused on his work, delivering packages all over town and beyond. Once, as he was about to leave a box on a front porch, the door opened, and there stood a young woman with a little girl at her side. Ben handed the woman the box and looked down at the girl, who eyed him cautiously.

"Thank you," the woman said.

But Ben couldn't speak. He hurried back to his truck, got in and sat there, sobbing. Through that doorway, the worst moment of his life had come rushing back.

Some minutes later, he was startled by a gentle knock on the door of his truck. It was the woman from the house.

"Are you okay?" she said.

Ben nodded yes, wiped his eyes and pulled away. He was too upset to keep working. He drove straight to his apartment, went inside and collapsed on his sofa. He lay there, remembering and weeping, for several hours before pulling himself together and driving his truck back to the distribution center.

That mother and child in Afghanistan were always in Ben's thoughts. He begged their forgiveness, but his pleas went unanswered. He was wracked with guilt. He wondered if it would ever go away.

One day, Ben read a news story about thousands of children in Afghanistan who had been left orphaned by the war. There was a photo of ragged children in a makeshift camp. Looking at it, Ben wondered if he might be able to adopt one of them.

He knew nothing could bring back the little girl whose life he had taken. But maybe he could rescue another child whose life hung in the balance.

He called an adoption agency in Davenport. The person there wasn't encouraging.

"Those adoptions can be complicated and take time," she said. "Maybe you'd like to consider adopting a child from Colombia or India instead."

"Thank you, but I'd really like to understand what it will take to adopt a child from Afghanistan," Ben said.

A week later, he met with the adoption agency in Davenport. A year later, after working with that agency and another in Kabul, a lawyer and the Veterans Administration and paying thousands of dollars, Ben was notified that his adoption application had been approved. He was thrilled.

The process, slow as it was, had actually been expedited because Ben had asked to adopt a young girl. Most adoptive parents want a baby and, in Afghanistan, girls are considered expendable.

The girl identified for adoption was three years old. Her name was Fatima. She was born in the eastern part of Afghanistan, not far from where Ben had seen action.

The agency in Kabul sent Ben her photo. She was tiny, with brown eyes and short black hair. She looked care-worn, but there was also a loveliness about her face.

"Fatima." Ben began saying her name and thinking about her not as an orphan in a distant land but as his daughter, a child who would soon be in his care.

On a Sunday morning, Ben stood holding a teddy bear in the baggage claim area of the airport in Des Moines. The adoption agency in Kabul had arranged for one of its workers named Noor to accompany Fatima from Kabul to Iowa. Noor was fluent in both Pashto and English.

Ben eagerly awaited Fatima's arrival. He'd been tracking her flight on his phone. It was running late. He prayed everything was okay. Maybe this is what it feels like to be a father, he thought.

Then, in a sea of passengers, he spotted a small girl in a pink skirt and a white blouse. He knew it was Fatima. She was looking around and holding the hand of a woman wearing a headscarf.

"Noor!" Ben called, waving his hand in the air.

He caught her eye, and the two of them started walking his way.

But as they came closer, another Afghan woman and child appeared in their place. Ben thought he was seeing things, but these two were as real as everyone around him. He had seen them before, in a room in ruins, in a moment of madness.

Now, though, they looked so serene. They were smiling. Their bodies were perfect. They were holding hands.

As they drew near, Ben expected them to say something, but they remained silent. For they had not come to tell him anything. They had come to bring him peace.

Somehow, Ben knew this, and his heart was filled with gratitude. He wanted to embrace them, but they faded away, just as Noor and Fatima reached him.

"Mr. Germain?" Noor said.

"Yes," Ben said, feeling like he were awakening from a dream.

"I am Noor. It is good to meet you."

Then she looked down at Fatima and said something in Pashto. The little girl looked up at Ben, smiled and said, "Ah bee."

"She says Daddy."

Ben got down on his knees.

"Hello, Fatima," he said softly.

Then father and daughter embraced. At last, both had been saved.

## Refuge

As a boy, Dylan would sometimes climb up to his treehouse to hide away from the things that upset him.

Once, after a particularly loud fight with his wife, Dylan's father Tom heard the backdoor slam and realized his eight-year-old son was gone.

"Where did Dylan go?" he asked his daughter, Lauren.

"He's up in his treehouse."

Tom went out into the backyard and stood at the base of a towering oak.

"Dylan!" he called.

"Yeah?"

"Can I come up?"

"I guess."

Tom had climbed the scrap wood "steps" up the trunk many times when he was building this treehouse. Since then, though, he hadn't been up there, and he'd put on a few pounds. Now, holding tight to the nailed-in boards above him and trying not to look down, he slowly made his ascent.

He found Dylan sitting in a corner with his hands wrapped around his knees. His eyes were red, like he'd been crying.

Tom lowered himself to the floor and sat in the opposite corner. Dylan was looking out the window.

"I'm sorry," Tom said. "I'm sorry that Mom and I were arguing."

Dylan looked down.

"Why do you and Mom fight so much?"

"Sometimes I do things and say things that make Mom upset, and sometimes she does and says things that make me upset. I wish we didn't."

"Then why do you?"

"It's hard to explain, and I know it's hard for you to understand."

"Don't you love Mom anymore?"

"I still love Mom. I'll always love her."

"Then why do you fight?"

"I don't know."

Then he said, "I'll try harder."

"No, you won't. You'll never stop fighting. Not until you and Mom get divorced."

"We're not going to get divorced, Dylan."

"Yeah, right."

Tom realized there was little he could say that would reassure his son. So he got up and said, "Come inside before it gets dark."

About a month later, Dylan's mother told Lauren and him that she and their father were getting a divorce. Lauren began crying. Dylan left and hid out in his treehouse for the rest of the afternoon.

When Dylan was 16, his mother died. By then, it was getting harder to climb up to his treehouse. So when bad things happened, things that upset him, he would take refuge in his bedroom. After the funeral, he spent the better part of three days there.

The following day, Tom and his wife Erin showed up — with a moving truck. They had decided to sell their house and move back into Tom's old house, the only house Dylan had ever known. His mother had paid it off.

Dylan and Erin weren't close. They hadn't been around each other much. When they were together, Dylan was cool to her. He didn't like the idea of another woman living with his father.

Living with Erin and Tom was a big change for Dylan. He'd lived with his mother and sister for nearly eight years. Now Lauren was away at college, and Erin's only child, Josh, was away at college too. All of sudden, Dylan felt like a stranger in his own home.

Despite his coolness toward Erin, though, she was kind to him. She seemed genuinely interested in his life. She prepared his favorite foods. She bought him a birthday present.

And Dylan began to warm to her. She was no substitute for his mother, but she offered a warmth he had never felt from his father.

Still, when something bad happened in his life, Dylan took to his bedroom. Once, during his junior year in high school, he holed up in there for a couple of days.

The first day, Erin gently knocked on his door to ask if he wanted dinner. He said he wasn't hungry, and she left him alone.

The second day, the same thing happened. Then Erin said, "May I come in?"

"Okay."

She opened the door. He was sitting on his bed. His eyes were red. The TV was on.

She stepped in and closed the door behind her. He grabbed the remote and turned off the TV.

"Are you okay?" she said.

"Yeah."

"Do you mind if I sit down?"

"Go ahead."

She stepped over to his desk, pulled out his chair and sat down.

"What's wrong?" she said.

He wasn't sure he wanted to tell her the truth, if he could trust her with the truth. But she seemed to really want to know. Besides, he had no one else to talk to.

"I asked a girl in my class to the prom, and she turned me down."

"I'm sorry."

He expected her to try to lift his spirits. Instead, she said, "Is that why you're in here?"

"Yeah," he said.

"So when you're upset, you stay in your room?"

"Yeah."

"I see," she said.

"When I was a kid, I used to go up into my treehouse in my backyard. My dad built it. But I haven't been up there for a long time. I'm not sure the steps will still hold me."

She smiled. He thought she might encourage him to face his fears. Instead, she said, "So your treehouse was your refuge, and now your bedroom is your refuge."

"Yeah."

"Bad things happen in our lives," she said. "I think it's important that we all have a place we can go to get away from whatever is upsetting us. By being here, you're taking care of yourself. I get it."

Dylan was stunned. As a kid, he had talked with his mother about hiding out in his treehouse. She had encouraged him to talk about his fears, but he'd never felt comfortable doing that. Eventually, hiding out, he began to feel guilty, like he was disappointing his mother. He still did it, but he felt suspect. He imagined his mother inside their house, shaking her head, wishing he would grow up.

But now Erin was saying hiding out was quite okay. He wasn't expecting that.

"Do you ever feel like hiding out?" he said.

"Oh, yeah. I always end up talking with your dad about what's bothering me. First, though, I usually go for a drive. It helps me to get away. It doesn't fix the problem, but it gives me some peace. You had your treehouse. Now you have your bedroom. I have my car. These are our places of refuge. We need them, and as long as we have them, I think we'll be okay."

Dylan blinked. That's exactly how he felt.

After that, his relationship with Erin changed. Dylan thought of her as a kindred spirit. He could never bring himself to call her mom. (Nor could his sister.) But now when he'd been in his bedroom for a while or she'd abruptly driven away, they talked. They helped each other heal.

Even when Dylan went away to college and he and Erin could no longer *see* when the other was hurting, once one of them had hidden away for a while, they would talk. For each of them, it was a great comfort to know that, on the other side of tough times, someone was there.

Dylan majored in business in college. After graduation, he got a job in marketing with a big company and moved away.

As he climbed the corporate ladder, the problems he faced became bigger, and they needed to be addressed, so Dylan could no longer simply hide away when something was upsetting him. He had to deal with bad news in real time.

But once he'd done that, on his own time, he would get away. He would always find a place where he could break free from his troubles, if only briefly. Then he would call Erin, and they would talk about it.

When Dylan got married, he would do the same with his wife, Emily. But Emily didn't take refuge from her own troubles. Erin was the only other person Dylan knew who did that.

When Dylan was 45, his father died suddenly of a heart attack. Emily and their children had never been close to his father, and Dylan decided to attend the funeral on his own.

The funeral and burial were small and simple, no-nonsense like Tom. Afterwards, Erin hosted a reception for family and friends at the house. Lauren and her husband were there as were Josh and his family. They all still lived close by and drove home after the reception.

Dylan had flown in. Erin insisted he stay with her rather than in a hotel. He was happy to be there for her and stay in his old house again.

Dylan arrived late the night before the funeral, so there was little time for him and Erin to talk then. That would have to wait.

Erin had been strong all day. But when everyone had left, she turned to Dylan and fell into his arms, sobbing. Finally, when she stopped crying, she said, "I need to go for a drive. Will you go with me?"

"Sure," he said.

It was getting dark, and she didn't like to drive at night anymore. So he drove.

"Where to?" he said.

"Anywhere."

Erin had driven around countless times after difficult experiences in her life. But she'd never had someone to talk with.

They talked mainly about Dylan's father. He asked her why she had married him.

"I was just coming off a terrible marriage," she said. "My first husband was abusive. Your father respected me, and he was good to Josh."

"Was he loving?"

"Not outwardly, no. He didn't show his emotions much. But he had a good heart."

"I guess."

"You needed affection, Dylan. Unfortunately, that's something Tom simply wasn't able to give you. But he loved you."

They were both silent for a minute. Then Dylan said, "You know, when Mom died and you and Dad moved in, I wasn't sure how I felt about that. Honestly, I wasn't sure how I felt about you. In hindsight, I was probably a jerk. But you were good to me and, in a way, you saved me. That night you came into my room, after I'd been turned down by that girl for the prom, I was crushed, and I wasn't sure I could go on. I think I needed someone to tell me it was okay to take a time out. Until then, I had told myself doing that was a sign of weakness. After that, I saw it as a sign of strength. I still do. That's made all the difference, and I have you to thank."

"I'm glad I could be there for you. And I have you to thank for always being there when I've needed someone to talk with as I've gone through my tough times."

They drove around for another hour, talking, saying nothing, just being there for one another.

When they got back, Dylan went up to his old room and closed the door. He opened the blinds and turned off the light so he could see into the backyard.

In the moonlight, through the leaves and limbs of the great oak, he could make out the contours of his old treehouse. He had taken refuge there so many times as a boy. Now he felt grateful to his father for making that possible.

## The Apostle

The Vatican, 2058

Angelo Salzano stepped into the forming line of old men wearing red robes and gold crosses and filed into the Sistine Chapel.

The 120 princes of the Catholic Church took their seats at four rows of tables. Each man then walked to the front and took an oath not to reveal what was about to happen.

A monsignor called out *"Extra omnes!"* — Latin for "Outside, all of you!" — and the massive double doors were closed, a key was turned and the conclave to choose a new pope was under way.

The presiding cardinal, Giuseppe Moretti, explained each step in the ancient ritual. Then each man wrote a few words in Latin on a rectangular piece of paper, "I elect as supreme pontiff ...," followed by his name.

One by one, they placed the paper on a gold saucer at the front of the room and tipped it into an urn. Then three cardinals, known as scrutineers, read out the name on each slip, keeping count of all the contenders.

From the start, three cardinals got the most votes: Kristof Nagy from Hungary, Jean Kapinga from Congo and Angelo Salzano from Genoa. Nagy was in the lead. However, none of them got close to the 80 votes required to secure the papacy.

The ballots were then stuffed into a cylindrical, cast-iron stove that had been installed by the main entrance of the chapel. Another stove next to it received chemicals to turn the smoke black. This is how thousands of people amassed in St. Peter's Square, and the world at large, learned a new pope had not yet been elected.

Later that afternoon, after a second round of voting, the same three cardinals remained the leading vote-getters. This time, though, Salzano took the lead. Still, black smoke signaled there would be no good news from the Vatican that day.

The following morning, in a third round of voting, Salzano got 84 votes. He had won. Inside the chapel, the cardinals rose and applauded. Outside, white smoke emerged, and the world cheered.

Salzano was stunned. He had never expected to become pope. He had been a longtime Vatican bureaucrat, a man who worked behind the scenes. Now he was the leader of the world's nearly two billion Catholics.

Cardinal Moretti stepped over to him and said, "Do you accept your canonical election as supreme pontiff?"

"Yes," Salzano said.

He then told Moretti the name he would assume, Francis III, and went to change into his newly tailored papal vestments in the Room of Tears, so named because many newly elected popes had wept there at the enormity of their task.

Now wearing his new vestments, Salzano returned to the Sistine Chapel. One by one, the cardinals approached him and pledged obedience.

Then he headed to the balcony of St. Peter's. Already there, Moretti proclaimed, "*Habeumus papam!* We have a pope!"

One hundred thousand people in St. Peter's Square below cheered as one.

"I present Angelo Salzano, Cardinal of the Holy Roman Church, who has taken the papal name Francis III."

Again, the crowd roared. Moretti then stepped aside, and Salzano appeared. Looking out at the sea of humanity, the new pope extended his right hand and, several times, made the sign of the cross.

A few minutes later, as the cheering and applause finally began to subside, Francis III leaned into a microphone and said, "Peace be with you."

The crowd fell silent.

"I am honored beyond words. My intention is simple: to continue the work of Pope Francesca to rededicate ourselves to following Jesus' great commandment. May God bless you all."

Then the new pope bowed and went inside.

In Sofia, Bulgaria, Cardinal Ivan Penov sat alone, watching the proceedings on a widescreen TV in his well-appointed apartment. Two years earlier, he had been forced to retire by Pope Francesca. He still hadn't forgiven her.

Now, listening to her successor's words, he muttered, "And your reign too will be brief."


Angelo Salzano, 68, had led the Roman Curia, the papal bureaucracy, for 11 years. He had been appointed by Pope Francis II. For the past three years, he had served in this role for Pope Francesca, the Catholic Church's first female pontiff.

Francesca, like her two immediate predecessors, Francis I and II, had been a reformer. But she had taken *her* idea of reform farther than any pope had in a century. Her vision for the Church was radical: to return to Jesus' great commandment to "love God and love your neighbor."

To determine *how* the Church would actually go about doing this, Francesca had convened Vatican III. Thousands of members of the clergy as well as lay people from all over the world had met over 18 months, following a process designed and led by Salzano.

But no sooner had Vatican III concluded than Pope Francesca died of a heart attack. The world mourned. Salzano was bereft. He considered Francesca the best leader he had ever known.

Working with Francesca had renewed Salzano. He was inspired by her simple vision for the Church and energized about helping make it a reality.

Now Francesca was gone, and the future of the Church was up to Francis III.

In his first official act as pope, Francis III called a news conference in the Vatican for that afternoon. Francesca had also called a news conference right away when she was elected pope. She wanted to be clear about her direction from the start. So did he.

Now reporters were gathered in the same, large conference room. At exactly 3:00 p.m., the new pope came in and stepped over to the podium.

At six feet, three inches tall, Francis III cut a very different figure than his diminutive predecessor. Like her, though, he had chosen to wear a simple white robe.

"Thank you for being here on short notice," he said. "I suppose this day is turning out a bit differently than any of us had planned."

Laughter rippled through the room.

The new pope had no notes, and there was no teleprompter.

"I just wanted to say just a few words about the direction of this papacy," he said. "Simply put, it will be dedicated to enacting the reforms called for by Vatican III. We will rededicate ourselves to bringing Jesus' teachings to life. We will focus on helping the poor and disadvantaged. And we will continue to flatten the structure of our Church and make it more inclusive.

"Pope Francesca was an extraordinary leader. She was also a woman of the world. She led with both eyes open. My eyes are open too. Change is never easy. I realize that following through on Vatican III will require us to change, as individuals and as a Church. And I know that real change will take time.

"Pope Francesca did not want to simply proclaim a new way for the Church, like some ancient decree. She wanted to engage Catholics around the world in a dialogue about how, together, we will advance our common mission. She was about to begin a global tour in St. Louis, Missouri, where she was from. I will follow in her footsteps and make a global tour of my own, beginning in my hometown of Genoa, here in Italy. Of course, no plans have yet been made, but I hope to begin soon. We'll be sharing details over the next few weeks.

"Finally, I would ask everyone for their prayers. Our Church is beginning anew. Our task is sacred. Our work will not be easy, but we enter into it with joyful hearts and full faith in God as the abiding and loving source of our strength. May God bless us all.

"Now, I'll be happy to take your questions."

Francis III had no illusions about the challenges he now faced. He knew that, while there was strong support for a more progressive Church, there was also growing resistance to this vision within the Church.

Surveys showed nearly 40 percent of Catholics felt the Church's reforms had gone too far. What's more, they believed the last few popes had led the Church in the wrong direction.

In their view, it was wrong to have allowed priests to marry and women to be ordained. Many felt the Church had become "too soft." Some wanted to bring back old traditions, from priests wearing cassocks to saying the Mass in Latin.

This far-right way of thinking had become a global movement. It even had a name: "The Right Way."

There was no single leader of this movement. However, one man's name was mentioned more than any other: Cardinal Ivan Penov. Officially, he was retired, but Penov had never let go of his right-wing followers. If anything, his forced retirement had increased his standing among them.

Francis III was realistic about his chances of changing hardline conservative Catholics' minds. But he saw himself as the leader of all Catholics, not just those who agreed with his more progressive vision for the Church. And he was hopeful that, by traveling the world as a personal ambassador for a more community-minded Church, he could at least solidify support for the reforms called for by Vatican III.

Yet Penov loomed in his mind. It was an open secret that he was behind an attempted assassination attempt on Pope Francesca, even though he was never charged with a crime. Now Francis III wondered if his life too was at risk.

But he would not let that stop him from taking his message to the people, and he tapped a small group from the Roman Curia to plan his global tour.

Their plan called for visiting 20 countries over three months. The pope would indeed begin in Genoa. From there, he would travel west.

Francis III would leave for Genoa in the spring, after tending to a range of official duties. Salzano had spent much of his career navigating bureaucracy. Now, as pope, he was swamped by it. By spring, he couldn't wait to get out of Rome.

His visit to Genoa would begin by celebrating an open-air Mass on the Piazza De Ferrari, the main square in the heart of the city.

Genoa had been a center of commerce in Italy since the Middle Ages. The tall buildings around the Piazza still housed many financial firms. Some had once been palaces. Others were modern office buildings. Genoa was a city both old and new.

Angelo Salzano's father had spent his career working as a banker in one of the older buildings. As a boy, Angelo would sometimes go with him to work. He was drawn to the elegant design of the offices and the refined way everyone dressed. He imagined himself working in such a place one day.

Like his father, Angelo had a mind for numbers. Early on, he decided he too would be a banker. In college, he majored in finance.

One summer, he interned with his father's firm. One morning, walking across the piazza on his way to work, Angelo came across a shabbily dressed man, sitting near the fountain, with a basket in front of him. He had always tried to avoid beggars, but he didn't see this one until he was nearly upon him.

"Buon giorno," the beggar said.

"Buon giorno," Angelo replied.

The beggar simply smiled at Angelo. Now feeling obliged to give him something, Angelo pulled out a five Euro note and dropped it in his basket.

He expected the beggar to say thank you. Instead, he said, "You are a man of God."

Angelo wasn't sure what to say, so he simply nodded and walked away.

At work that day, Angelo couldn't stop thinking about what the beggar had said. How did he know this? Angelo didn't *feel* like a man of God. He'd been raised Catholic but didn't consider himself religious. He no longer even attended Mass on Sundays.

After work, Angelo stopped into the Church of San Pancrazio at the edge of the piazza. The church was small. There were no pews, only chairs. Angelo sat down. Looking around, he contrasted the church's simplicity with the finely wrought features of his father's workplace. The elegance and opulence of those offices had once been so alluring to him. But now, immersed in it every day, he had begun to feel differently. The cherry wood paneling, the wool carpeting, the ebony desks had lost their appeal, as had the prospect of spending his life as a banker.

Angelo felt lost. For the first time, he questioned his path. He wasn't sure where he belonged or what he should be doing. Then he thought again about what the beggar had said. "You are a man of God." Maybe I am, he thought. Maybe I'm being called to a different kind of life.

Angelo had never thought about becoming a priest. But now, he was intrigued by the idea. He returned to college in the fall, but the more he studied business, the less it appealed to him — and the more he thought about a religious life.

Over the Christmas holiday, his parents were shocked when Angelo announced he wanted to suspend his university studies and enter the seminary.

"Wonderful!" his mother said.

"Why don't you think about this a bit more?" said his father. "Finish this school year. Then you can decide."

He followed his father's advice. By summer, his calling felt stronger than ever. That fall, to his mother's delight and his father's chagrin, Angelo entered the seminary.

From the start, it felt like the right place for him. The structured regimen fit with his disciplined nature. He found theology and philosophy fascinating and refreshing. And the more he saw the kind of work priests were doing, the more Angelo felt called to such a ministry.

Now, nearly 50 years later, Angelo Salzano had become Pope Francis III. It had all begun for him that morning on the Piazza De Ferrari. So he knew that is where he must begin his world tour as pope.

It was a warm and brilliant spring day in Genoa. The piazza was filled with people, who surrounded the stage that had been constructed for the pope to celebrate Mass.

Signs and banners waved throughout the crowd. Many welcomed Francis III home. Some, though, were a reminder of the opposition he faced. "Jesus wept," said one. "Bring back Benedict," said another.

Just after noon, Francis III stepped up the pulpit and began his homily.

"My brothers and sisters," he said with a broad smile. "It is so good to be home."

The crowd cheered wildly, and the pope pivoted, waving to his fellow Genoese all around him. It was a scene of joy and sweet communion.

Except for two men with rifles. Each of them crouched low behind slightly opened windows on the upper floors of two tall buildings. Each had Francis III in the crosshairs of his scope. Each was wearing an earpiece.

"Now," said a voice in their ears.

Each man squeezed the trigger on his gun, and two shots rung out. At that very moment, the pope had turned to face the people behind him. Then his body jerked sideways, as if someone had pushed him, and he fell to his left.

A priest close to him watched in horror as Francis III hit the wooden floor hard. He lay there, not moving. Blood seeped through his white robe and pooled around his upper body and head. The cleric knelt beside him but wasn't sure what to do.

"Help!" he cried. "Help!"

By then, security guards and police had rushed onto the stage and surrounded the pope, facing outward, their rifles and handguns drawn. One policeman spoke into a walkie talkie on his shoulder. A siren blared.

The stunned crowd was hushed. People could no longer see Francis III. They weren't sure what had happened, but they feared the worst. "No!" someone shouted. People were crying. Some knelt and prayed.

Now medics were on the stage, examining the pope. They called for a stretcher, and two men rushed up the stairs with one. They carefully lifted the pope onto it, and four men slowly carried him down. A few minutes later, the piercing sound of an ambulance siren began to fade.

Everything was confusion. No one made an announcement. Some police ushered people from the piazza while others ran into several of the surrounding buildings and began looking for shooters.

Five hours later, Pope Francis III lay in bed in the International Evangelical Hospital, unconscious after surgery. He had been hit near his left shoulder. The bullet had shattered his collarbone. Fortunately, it had missed vital organs, though it came dangerously close to his carotid artery.

A second shot had missed the pope altogether. Unfortunately, it had hit a woman standing in the crowd. Tragically, it killed her instantly.

Within an hour of the shooting, police had discovered and apprehended two gunmen. Each was hiding on the top floor of a building. They had hidden there overnight and managed to elude a final security search of all the buildings around the piazza that morning.

The men were Bulgarian. Even before they were interrogated, authorities in Sofia were knocking on the door of Cardinal Ivan Penov's apartment.

Pope Francis III was a strong man. Within a few days, he was able to get out of bed and walk around his hospital room. But he would not be able to return to Rome for a month, and his full recovery would take another month beyond that.

News of the assassination attempt sparked an outpouring of prayers and well wishes from around the world. The pope was grateful — and he hoped the goodwill would translate into support for Vatican III.

For a while, it did. Francis III's global tour would have to be postponed. But from a meeting room in the hospital, he began to conduct video calls with groups of Catholics in the countries he had planned to visit. He held these calls every few days. When he returned to Rome, he continued them, eventually meeting virtually with Catholics in all 20 of the countries on his scheduled tour.

News coverage of these calls was generally positive, and it helped create enthusiasm for the reforms of Vatican III. As the pope recovered physically, his spirits were buoyed by stories of Catholics all around the world doing so much more to help the poor and disadvantaged in their communities. Clearly, efforts to make the Church more externally focused were working.

He was also pleased by plans developed by a small working group of the Roman Curia to reduce the number of dioceses and archdioceses globally from 3,000 to 2,000 over five years. This streamlining would save enormous time, money and effort and push decision-making down to the local level, where clergy and lay people best know what's needed.

And he was excited that a small group of clergy and lay people were working on recommendations for making the Church more inclusive. They promised recommendations soon.

Francis III confided in his old friend Cardinal Giovanni Luciani, "It is doubtful we'd be making such strong progress if I hadn't been shot."

"I don't know about that, Angelo. I'm just glad you're okay."

But there were distressing signs too. The Right Way was capitalizing on all the attention being paid to the reforms of Vatican III to rally ultraconservative Catholics in protesting those very reforms.

The likelihood that the Church would soon sanction same-sex marriage was a particular flashpoint for many. Francis III had privately signaled his support for same-sex marriage. Pope Francesca had been supportive too, though she stopped short of tackling that divisive issue to help ensure broad support for Vatican III.

Now that Vatican III was rolling out, Francis III intended to issue an encyclical on same-sex marriage and use that as a basis for officially including gays and lesbians in the Church, a move he felt was long overdue.

The pope held this close, but there are no secrets in the Vatican. Rumors that the Church would soon be "defiled" incensed hardline Catholics around the world, especially in Asia and Africa, where the Church, like the world, was growing fastest.

There was open talk of a schism within the Church. Some ultraconservatives had even begun calling their faction "The True Church."

Such talk was unsettling to Francis III, and he felt a need to counter it. He turned to a small group of trusted advisors, including Luciani, for guidance.

Their counsel was to fortify support for Vatican III in more progressive countries and communities and try to build alliances with conservative Catholics around common-ground issues, such as homelessness.

Francis III listened carefully but pushed back.

"It sounds like a recipe for further division," he said. "We need to convert hearts and minds."

"Your Holiness," Luciani said, "the growing rightward movement within the Church is not happening in a vacuum. It is part of a broader movement among people and nations everywhere."

"Is that so?"

"Yes, Your Holiness," Luciani continued. "There are more autocratic regimes in place now than there have been since the Second World War. But unlike in the twentieth century, many people today seem quite okay with autocracy. It's a sad fact, but one we must acknowledge."

"And so we should simply acquiesce?"

"No, your Holiness. We believe, as you do, in the reforms called for by Vatican III. We also believe that, over time, your more progressive vision for the Church will prevail. That's why we're recommending pressing ahead."

Francis III sat back in his chair and sighed.

"What is Cardinal Penov's role in all of this?"

The pope's advisors looked at each other and said nothing.

"Your Eminence?" the pope finally said, looking at Luciani.

"Your Holiness, Cardinal Penov has maintained active communication with certain conservative cardinals around the world."

"Is he encouraging them to oppose Vatican III?"

Again, the advisors said nothing.

The pope looked Luciani in the eye.

"Gianni?"

"Your Holiness," he said, "Penov's role in this movement cannot be underestimated."

Francis III blinked, taking that in.

"Thank you for your candor," he said to the group, "and your excellent advice. I hope I can continue to count on you."

"Yes," they all said.

"Thank you. I will be calling on you again soon."

Sensing the meeting was over, the advisors got up to leave.

"Your Eminence," the pope said to Luciani, "will you stay for a minute?"

"Of course, Your Holiness."

When the others had gone, Francis III turned to his friend and said, "I want to meet with Penov."

"For what purpose?"

"I want to hear the truth from him."

"And then what, Angelo? Do you expect him to back down?"

"I don't know. But if he is indeed organizing a movement that is tearing our Church apart, I must try."

"Your Holiness, Penov is not the source of division within our Church. He is merely stirring the pot."

"I know, Gianni. But after all he has done, including orchestrating the attempted assassination of two popes, it is time he stop stirring."

Francis III summoned Penov and arranged to meet with him in a conference room in the Apostolic Palace. The pope made sure the cardinal was there before he entered the room. He wanted to remind Penov who was in charge.

"Your Holiness," Penov said, standing up as the pope came in.

"Your Eminence, welcome."

Francis III stepped in and stood at the end of the conference table. He wanted Penov to come to him. When Penov reached him, the pope held out his hand. Penov took it, bent down and kissed his ring. It was an old tradition Francis III didn't normally follow. Now, though, he would make an exception.

"Sit," he said, extending his hand.

Penov took a seat near him.

"How may I be of service, Your Holiness?"

"I will get to that in a moment. First, though, I have a question."

"Yes, Your Holiness?"

"Is it true you have been in touch with certain cardinals around the world?"

"I'm not sure I understand."

"Then let me be clearer. Have you encouraged more conservative cardinals of the Church to oppose the reforms called for by Vatican III?"

Penov looked surprised.

"Your Holiness ..."

The pope leaned forward.

"Answer me."

Penov leaned back in his chair and folded his hands on his lap.

"Yes, I have."

Now the pope was surprised. He was not expecting such candor from Penov.

"Why?"

"I believe the Church has veered too far left."

"I'm sure you do believe that," the pope said, his voice beginning to rise. "But does that give you the right to encourage, if not organize, opposition to reforms which have been thoughtfully and prayerfully called for by a Vatican Council?"

"Your Holiness, I might be retired, but I am still a cardinal in our Church. I see it as my duty to speak out against wrongs wherever I see them."

"And you think Vatican III is wrong?"

"Yes, I do. Frankly, I think it is liberalism run amok."

"I see. Your Eminence, let me ask you something. When you were ordained, did you take a vow of obedience?"

"Yes, I did."

"Well, I am giving you an order. From now on, you are to have no contact with any cardinal, archbishop or bishop of the Church."

"No contact?"

"None at all, directly or indirectly."

"Your Holiness, with respect, that seems extreme."

"Is it any more extreme than attempting to assassinate a pope?"

Penov looked away.

"And what if I choose to disobey this order?"

"Then you will be excommunicated."

"I see," Penov said, his face now red. "Well, Your Holiness, that will not be necessary. I will have no other contact with any of my peers."

"Or archbishops or bishops."

"Or archbishops or bishops."

After an awkward silence, Penov said, "Will there be anything else, Your Holiness?"

"No, Your Eminence. But know that, should you disobey my order, I *will* find out."

"I understand," Penov said, looking chastened.

Naturally, word got out about Francis III's meeting with Penov. Just as the pope had expected, reprimanding Penov led those on the far right to take an even harder line against Vatican III.

Some began to vilify Francis III too. Many called him a leftist and a bleeding-heart liberal. Some even called him the anti-Christ.

But the pope didn't care. All he cared about was seeing further progress in rolling out the reforms of Vatican III.

When his working group recommended allowing gays and lesbians to join the Church and sanctioning same-sex marriage, Francis III waited a few weeks, then issued an encyclical entitled "Una Familia" or One Family. In it, he cited Jesus' acts of compassion toward the marginalized of his day.

"Jesus is our role model," the encyclical stated. "He was inclusive. We, his disciples, must be inclusive too."

This set The Right Way on its ear. But when Francis III then ruled to officially welcome homosexuals into the Church and expand the sacrament of matrimony to include same-sex couples, the ultraconservative movement to split from the Church went into overdrive.

The pope shuddered at the idea of a schism. But he continued to believe in the reforms of Vatican III, and he had full faith that, as a more progressive Church took shape, people would join in the work to bring Jesus' teachings to life.

"We must get back to our original purpose," he said. "The Church must be renewed."

But in the coming months and years, the division within the Church became more pronounced. The Right Way even created an organization whose sole purpose was to form a new church.

Francis III did all he could to prevent a split, including traveling to meet conservative Church leaders and members on their turf. While most of them appreciated this outreach, the hardliners dug in all the more.

Then Francis III, whose health had always seemed so robust, fell ill. He tired easily now and began to lose weight. Some had seen him wince in pain.

He went to a hospital for tests, which revealed he had late-stage pancreatic cancer. His doctors gave him months to live. He declined treatment.

Then, almost overnight, the calls for a new church went silent.

At first, the pope was encouraged. Maybe, he thought, the outpouring of sympathy for him would lead to more support for Vatican III.

But then he realized his adversaries had gone quiet because they knew they might finally be able to elect a like-minded pope. There would be no need for a schism now. Under the right leader, they could slow-walk Vatican III and bring back "real Catholicism."

Francis III wanted to reach out to those cardinals who would soon be forming a new conclave with a plea that they elect a pope who would continue to reform the Church. But he knew that would only interfere and probably not change many minds anyway.

So in his remaining time, the pope chose to personally show the way. Though weak, he fed people in soup kitchens and visited people in homeless shelters, hospitals and prisons throughout Rome. He talked with people in the streets, met them where they were. He gave money to beggars.

Cardinal Luciani was chosen to preside over Francis III's funeral Mass in St. Peter's Basilica. It was packed with religious leaders and dignitaries from around the world.

"He was on a path to be a banker," Luciani said in his homily. "Instead, Angelo Salzano listened to a poor man and became a man of God."

Then he turned and faced the section of the church where his fellow cardinals were seated, a sea of red.

"May we continue to take inspiration from a poor man too," he said. "For we are, as he told us, the light of the world."

## Long Way Home

Lee Parker, senior executive with Boston Bank, was a man with secrets.

For starters, Lee was his middle name. His first name was Colton. He told everybody he was from Boston. In fact, he was from Cordele, Georgia, the poorest town in the state. Everyone there called him Colt.

His refined ways were the product of studying his professors and classmates at Harvard and imitating the way they talked, dressed, walked, laughed and even combed their hair.

Lee grew up on a farm whose main crop was watermelons. There were many watermelon farms in Cordele, which called itself "the watermelon capital of the world." Cordele watermelons were known for being round, very sweet and very juicy. People loved them. At harvest time, they were sold all over southwestern Georgia. Some people even came over from Alabama and up from Florida to buy them.

Growing watermelons was a way for Lee's father, an uneducated man, to make a living and provide for his family. The Parkers lived just above the poverty line, although sometimes just below it. Their house was small. They had one car, an old Chevy, but they hardly ever went anywhere as a family, except for church every Sunday.

Lee had two brothers and one sister. He shared a tiny bedroom with his two brothers. His sister slept in a hall closet that had been converted into a "bedroom."

Every spring, summer and fall, Lee and his brothers worked the fields with their father. It was back-breaking work, and Lee hated it. He hated being poor too. For him, poverty was a source of shame, even at school, where most of the other kids were from poor families too.

Lee dreamed of breaking free from his poor existence. He dreamed of being rich, of having nice things, of living in a big city, where people had good jobs, lived in beautiful houses and drove expensive cars.

"I'm gonna get outta here," he told his brother Earl as they harvested watermelons one day.

"Where you gonna go?"

"College."

Earl laughed.

"Right," he said. "And how you gonna do that?"

"I'm gonna get a scholarship."

"How?"

"Mrs. Beckman told me that, with my grades and Daddy's low income, I can apply to any college I want, and there's a good chance I'll qualify for all kinds of aid," Lee said. "Scholarships too."

"So where you gonna apply?"

"Harvard."

Earl spit out the water he was drinking.

"Harvard! Colt, you are a dreamer. You get into Harvard, and I'll eat this here watermelon whole."

"You're on," said Lee.

In his junior year in high school, with the help of Mrs. Beckman, the school counselor, Lee began applying to a range of universities, including Harvard. In his applications, he made it clear he would need financial aid and that he was interested in any scholarships that were available.

In university parlance, Lee was known as a marginalized candidate. All the universities where he applied expressed interest because they were all on the lookout for disadvantaged prospects.

But the school Lee was most keenly interested in was Harvard. He knew that with a Harvard degree, he could do about anything. It might be a long shot, but at 17, Lee had decided to shoot for the stars.

When he received a conditional offer of admission from Harvard, with the promise of financial aid and scholarships, Lee was ecstatic.

With Mrs. Beckman's help once again, Lee quickly filled out all the forms requested by Harvard. In March of his senior year, he received an acceptance. By May, he had secured all the financial assistance he would need to attend Harvard in the fall.

"Eat up," he said to Earl, handing him a big, round watermelon.

The summer after he graduated from high school, Lee dedicated himself to three things: learning all he could about Harvard and Boston; listening to newscasters and movie stars talk, imitating their accents and dropping his southern drawl; and making enough money to buy dental veneers for his "smile teeth." Lee had never been to a dentist, and his teeth were a mess.

That August, when the watermelons on his father's farm were at their ripest, Lee left for Boston with nearly everything he owned packed in one suitcase.

At the bus station, his mother sobbed, and his father was stoic.

"Come home at Christmas," his father said, shaking Lee's hand.

"I will, Daddy."

But Lee did not come home that Christmas or for the next four years or even after he got a job at Boston Bank.

By the time he graduated from Harvard, Lee had fully adopted a Boston accent and dropped all traces of his southern heritage. Tall, handsome and well-spoken, he had a refined air about him. He had majored in finance and interned with firms in Boston every summer during college. They all offered him jobs. His senior year, he interviewed with a dozen firms and took the best offer — from Boston Bank.

His rise there was meteoric. By 30, Lee was running one of the bank's practice groups. By 40, he was a vice president and on everyone's short list of candidates for CEO.

When he was 28, he met a red-headed beauty named Rachel at a party. They were immediately attracted to one another, and he asked her out that night. She said yes, and they started dating.

At first, when Rachel asked him about where he was from, Lee would say, "Nowhere special. I'll tell you about it sometime."

But after several of these dodges and once they'd fallen in love, Rachel pressed him.

"Lee, I really want to know. It's important."

They were having lunch at the kitchen table in her apartment.

"Okay," Lee said, tipping back the last of his iced coffee. "Let's go in your living room."

They went in and sat on the sofa. Her expression was a mix of intrigue and anxiety.

"I have to ask you to keep what I'm about to tell you in strictest confidence," he said.

"Lee," she said with a small laugh, "you're scaring me."

He reached out for her hand.

"Don't worry," he said. "There's nothing to be afraid of."

"Oh, good," she said, bringing her hand to her chest. "Yes, I'll keep it in confidence."

"Thank you. Here's the truth."

He proceeded to tell Rachel everything. She listened carefully, saying nothing. He wasn't sure how to read her. He imagined she might get up at any moment and kick him out.

But when he'd finished, she took his hand and said, "Thank you for sharing that. I know how hard it was for you. I just want you to know I love you. I will always love you."

He was so surprised and relieved that his eyes welled with tears. She scooted over and wrapped her arms around him.

"Why have you been hiding your past?" she said.

"Because I'm ashamed of it."

"Why?"

"Because people would think I'm a hillbilly. Because they'd think I'm a fraud. Because it would kill my career."

"Lee," she said with a smile, "anyone who knows you respects you. No one would think less of you if they knew where you were from. If anything, they might think even more of you."

"They can never know," he said.

"Well, I'll never say a word. But eventually, people are going to find out."

"Why do you say that? I've been in Boston for years, and no one here has a clue."

"Yeah, but ..."

"But what?"

"Well, what if we get married? What if we have kids? Won't you want to share that with your parents? With your brothers and sister?"

"No," he said flatly.

"No? How can say that? Don't you love them?"

He stood up and began pacing.

"I do love them, but that's beside the point.

"Well, what is the point?"

"The point is: that part of my life is gone. It's gone forever. I've dreamed about a life and a place like this since I was a boy. And now my dream is coming true, Rachel. This is where I belong. Cordele doesn't exist for me anymore, and the boy who grew up there doesn't exist anymore either."

Now Rachel looked concerned.

"Are you saying you'll never go back to Cordele again?"

"That's right."

"But Lee, what if we get married? Wouldn't you want your family to come to the wedding?"

"No."

She shook her head.

"This doesn't make any sense."

He stopped pacing and looked at her.

"I knew I shouldn't have told you."

"Lee! I have no problem with the fact that you grew up poor, and I can understand why you've changed. But cutting your family off ... I guess I just don't get it."

"I knew you wouldn't understand."

"Lee? Now you really are scaring me."

"Don't worry."

"Don't worry? But you've just told me if we got married, you wouldn't even invite your family to our wedding and that we'd have to keep your past a deep, dark secret. Lee, no matter how you feel about your childhood, that's just not right."

"Well, then, maybe ... maybe we don't belong together."

"What?"

"I said ..."

"I know what you said. I think you should leave. I think you should think hard about what you've told me today."

"Okay."

He started walking to the door. She began to follow him, but he turned and said, "I'll let myself out."

Lee knew he was screwed. He knew that if he didn't tell Rachel he'd be open about his background and reconnect with his family, it would be over between them.

Lee wondered if he was being unreasonable. Maybe I'm well established and successful enough here that revealing my past won't matter, he thought.

But he couldn't rid himself of the feeling of shame he associated with his poor roots. He couldn't shake the fear that he would be a laughingstock if people knew the truth, if they knew he had grown up tending watermelons.

The following day, he texted Rachel to see if could drop by after work that evening. She said yes.

She assumed he had come to apologize. But he had come to ask if *she* had reconsidered.

"No," she said.

"Well, then —"

"Lee! Don't do this! I love you. This is all so silly."

"It's not silly to me."

She started crying. But instead of trying to console her, Lee walked to the door and simply said, "Goodbye."

He vowed not to get romantically involved with a woman again. He knew any girlfriend would want to know about his past. She would want to meet his parents. She would want their children to know their grandparents.

He knew that Rachel had not been unreasonable. But he just couldn't risk the exclusive world he was now a part of learning of his past.

He began having a recurring nightmare that he was in the middle of a big presentation to a major client and his dental veneers fell off. Everyone in the room started laughing at him. Embarrassed, he ran out, and when he stopped running, he was back in Cordele, standing in a field, still wearing a suit, cutting watermelon vines.

He would wake up sweating and shaking. Every time he had that dream, he became a little more resolved to keep his past a secret.

One Monday morning, when he was 42, Lee was in a staff meeting in his conference room when his secretary came in and whispered something in his ear.

"Excuse me," he said. "Keep going. I'll be right back."

It was his sister, Maddie. She had never called him, so he knew it was serious.

"It's Daddy," she said. "He's gone."

Lee decided he had to attend the funeral. But he didn't tell anyone, not even his secretary, why he was taking the rest of the week off. He flew into Atlanta and rented a car for the two-hour drive south to Cordele.

He parked in the gravel driveway of his old house, walked up the stone path to the front door and knocked.

A sturdy, middle-aged woman opened the door. He didn't recognize her at first. But then she said, "Oh, Colt," and he knew from her sweet voice it was his sister.

"I'm sorry, Maddie," he said, stepping inside and embracing her.

He heard footsteps and looked up. There was his mother. He could hardly believe how old she looked. When he'd last seen her, she was middle-aged, with flecks of gray in her auburn hair. Now her hair was white, and she looked so thin and frail.

He let go of Maddie and stepped over to his mother.

"Mama," he said, embracing her.

"Oh, Colt."

Then she began sobbing, and he remembered how she had cried like that the last time he'd seen her, when she and his father had seen him off to college.

"I'm sorry, Mama," he said.

And he was sorry. Sorry for the loss of his father. Sorry he had been away so long. Sorry he had not been a dutiful son.

He sat in the family room with his mother and sister, who sat next to each other on the sofa. Though he was seldom at a loss for words, Lee wasn't sure where to begin.

"Daddy was out in the field, tending the watermelons," Maddie said, breaking the awkward silence. "It was a heart attack."

His mother wiped her eyes with a white handkerchief with red embroidery at the edges. Lee remembered it from his childhood.

"I'm sorry," Lee said. "Thank you for calling me."

Lee spent the rest of the week in Cordele. He slept in his old room, which still had three single beds in it. He got reacquainted with his brothers, both of whom still lived in Cordele, and met his nieces and nephews.

Everyone was polite, though not warm. He realized these people no longer really knew him and how strange he must seem to them.

His father's funeral at the First Presbyterian Church was packed. Lee recognized some parishioners, although everyone looked so much older, and many looked ill. It was a reminder of how hard life was in Cordele and how it wore people down. It was a reminder of why he had left.

But there were more pleasant moments that week too. Maddie, Earl and Lee's other brother Emmett had Lee and their mother over to their houses for dinner, and they shared lots of stories shared from Lee's childhood. He'd forgotten most of them or at least put them away.

Now hearing these stories, Lee was mindful that, while his family might have been poor, they had lots of fun too. He had forgotten that part.

The day before he left, Lee went out into the fields. Walking through the rows of soybeans, peanuts and watermelons, the sweet, strong scent of the red earth rose up and filled his nostrils. He had forgotten all about it.

He knelt down and ran his hand over the smooth rind of a small watermelon. How many of these I tended, he thought. How many vines I cut. Working these fields had been a big part of his young life.

He had grown to hate it, but now he also remembered how much he loved biting into one of these sweet melons and how the juice would run down his neck and cool him on a hot summer afternoon. He had forgotten that part too.

Before he left, Lee promised his mother he would call or write her every week. He would have preferred to text her, but she didn't have a cell phone. As he made her that promise, she smiled. It was the first time that week he had seen his mother smile, and he glimpsed true joy in her eyes.

When he returned to Boston, Lee made good on his promise to his mother. Not only that, but he came back to Cordele that Christmas, finally making good on what he'd told his father the last time he'd seen him.

By 43, Lee was a lock to be Boston Bank's new CEO, and the company decided it was time to begin raising his public profile, especially in Boston. Lee joined several boards and got involved in a couple of highly visible community projects.

One was a new community garden in the city, just a few blocks from the bank's main offices in the Prudential Building. One spring morning, Lee attended an event to dedicate the "green" space, which was actually a city block covered with dirt where dilapidated buildings had once stood.

"What will you grow here?" Lee asked the project leader, a pretty, 30-something woman named Emily Dodd.

"Asparagus, tomatoes, blueberries, potatoes and pumpkins," she said. "And flowers, of course."

"How about watermelons?"

"Well, we hadn't thought of watermelons. I guess we could grow those too."

"I'll make you a deal," Lee said. "You set aside space for watermelons, and I'll buy the seeds, plant them and take care of the watermelons all summer. I'll even harvest them. All you'll need to do is keep them watered."

Emily looked at Lee and smiled, no doubt amused by the idea that this business executive in a tailored suit was going to get down on his hands and knees and tend watermelons.

"You're on," she said.

That evening, Lee went online and ordered a bag of "icebox watermelon" seeds. They arrived a few days later. That Saturday, when he knew Emily would be at the site, he put on jeans and work boots, grabbed a hoe, a trowel and a pair of work gloves he'd also bought that week and headed downtown.

He parked in his space in the Prudential Building garage. He knew some Boston Bank employees came into the office on Saturdays and thought someone might see him. But he didn't care. If anyone asked, he was simply helping tend a garden the bank had underwritten.

When he got to the garden, Emily was there. She looked surprised to see him, as if she didn't think he would actually show up.

"Mr. Parker, it's so good to see you again."

"It's good to be here. Please call me Lee."

"Okay, Lee. Let me show you the area I set aside for your watermelons."

She showed him a section she'd roped off.

"How big is that?" Lee said.

"Fifteen by 15."

"Hmmm."

"What?"

"Could you give me a few more feet?"

"Sure," she said. "Why?"

"I'd like to plant three rows, and they need to be six feet apart."

"No problem. You can have a few more feet over here."

"Thanks," he said, setting down the bag of seeds and his tools.

"Need any help?" she said.

"No, thanks. I think I've got this."

"It looks like you do," she said with a smile.

Using his hoe, Lee formed three, 12-inch-tall hills of soil, spaced six feet apart. Using his trowel, he planted eight seeds along each hill. Then he stood back and looked at his handiwork.

Emily had been watching him.

"That's it?" she said.

"Yeah, for now."

"What I mean is, I thought you'd be planting a lot more seeds."

"Just wait. In a month, this whole area will be covered with vines."

"Cool," she said. "I take it you've done this before.

"Once or twice."

"Well, I'll be watering everything that's planted this afternoon. I'll make sure your watermelon seeds get plenty of water."

"Thank you," he said. "I might come back tomorrow morning to check on them."

"I'll be here."

"Good."

When he came back the following morning, Emily was standing in the center of all the dirt, working it with a hoe.

"Good morning, Emily," he called.

"Good morning, Lee," she said, walking over.

She looked different. She was wearing khaki pants instead of jeans and a more form-fitting T-shirt, and her hair, which was usually pulled back, now fell down around her shoulders. Lee had thought Emily was attractive in a mother-earth sort of way. Now, he couldn't take his eyes off her.

"Do you ever take a break?" he said.

"Yeah, often."

"Well, when you're ready for a break, can I buy you a cup of coffee?"

"How about now?" she said, taking off her work gloves.

He noticed she wasn't wearing a wedding ring.

Over coffee, he asked her to dinner the following Saturday. She said yes. When he picked her up, she was wearing a floral-patterned sundress. It showed off her youthful figure.

"So how it is you know so much about growing watermelons?" she said over a glass of wine.

In that moment, Lee thought of his father and mother, his brothers and sister, his nieces and nephews. He thought of Cordele and how, as much as he had tried to bury his past, it was a part of him, a part he no longer felt he needed to hide.

"I grew up on a farm," he said with a smile.

# Flash Fiction

## Grow

Nick Reynolds, legendary food industry veteran, had just begun a special assignment with his longtime employer, Elgin Foods. The final two years of his career were to be spent reinvigorating Elgin's stale corporate strategy and making sure the right people were in place to lead the company forward.

It was a plum assignment. It was also a way for Nick to save face and exit gracefully after years of bullying people had nearly cost him his job.

Fortunately for Nick, he had an advocate in Lou Bradford, Elgin's CEO. Nick's business results were unmatched. He had built Elgin's snack cakes business into a world beater. Bradford was reluctant to simply let such a strong performer go. But he also genuinely believed Nick was well qualified for this assignment. He knew Elgin's business and its people well.

Or so Bradford thought.

"These people are crazy," Nick told him after his first week in his new role.

"What?"

"The whole lot of them."

"Who?"

"Our general managers, the ones you think should be running this company for the next 20 years."

"Why do you say that?"

"Well, for starters, most of them don't think we should even be in the snack cakes business."

"Why?"

"It's not healthy."

"What? It's our healthiest business by far."

"I mean they feel our products aren't good for you. They think we should be selling more nutritious foods."

"Maybe they're right."

"But it doesn't stop there, Lou. They think our packaging should be environmentally friendly and our plants should run on renewable energy. They want us to reduce our carbon footprint."

"Well, we do have room to improve."

"Improve? Hell, Lou. They want us to save the damn planet!"

Bradford smiled. Nick gave him a curious look.

"Sorry, Nick. But it just occurred to me these people don't report to you anymore. They're probably just speaking their minds."

"Maybe so. But have you met with these folks lately, Lou?"

"Not as much as I'd like."

"Well, good luck finding them."

"What do you mean?"

"I mean they all work from home now. When I ask them to come into the office to meet, they act put out."

"Well, after Covid, we did let everyone work remotely a few days a week."

"I know, but I'm not sure how much they're working at all. They seem a lot more interested in making sure their teams are diverse than actually getting work done. And have you seen how they dress?"

"It's a new world, Nick. Younger people don't think about work the way we have."

"But who's going to actually do the work, Lou? Who's going to lead Elgin forward when people like us are gone?"

Bradford sat back in his chair, closed his eyes and pressed his fingertips against the bridge of his nose.

"Look, Nick, I need you to do something for me."

"What's that?"

"I need you to put aside the past and try to see things as they are. The world has changed, and these younger people aren't like us. If we're going to have a thriving business tomorrow, we need to take a good look at the world and where it's going, and we need to listen to the people who are going to take us there."

"But Lou —"

Bradford held up his hand.

"Nick, I gave you this assignment because I thought you could do it. I still think you can do it. But only if you change. Don't expect the future leaders of this company to be like you. You don't have to agree with them, but you should respect them. You have to take time to understand where they're coming from. They're not crazy, Nick. You just need to hear them out. You've been in this job for a week. I want you to come back to me in six months and deliver on what you signed up for. But to do that, you're going to have to start listening to people. You're going to have to change."

Nick couldn't believe what he was hearing. He thought Bradford would be sympathetic.

"Nick?"

"What?"

"Are you still in?"

Nick thought for a moment.

"What are my options?"

Looking him in the eye, Bradford said, "Grow or retire."

Nick blinked and sat back in his chair.

"Can I have some time to think about it?"

"No, Nick. I need your answer now."

Nick looked over at a display of vintage Elgin products. Jim Edwards came to mind. He had been a senior vice president at Elgin when Nick was a young manager. Nick was struggling and about to quit. But Edwards saw his potential and saved him.

Edwards went on to mentor Nick until he retired. Ultimately, he learned as much from Nick as Nick did from him.

Nick turned back to Bradford.

"Grow," he said.

## The Secret

As a girl, when Marie experienced discomfort, her mother would retrieve a cobalt blue cruet, uncork it and sprinkle droplets of water wherever her daughter was ailing.

Each time, Marie's pain would subside.

The little girl was amazed.

"What is that, Mama?"

"Holy water."

"Where did you get it?"

"It's been in our family for generations. My mother sprinkled it on me when I was a girl, and my grandmother sprinkled it on my mother when she was a girl."

"Where did it come from?"

"France, where your great grandmother was born."

"What makes it holy?"

Her mother smiled.

"Someday, I'll tell you."

Marie didn't press, but she stayed curious. She'd heard about the holy water of Lourdes and how people claimed to have been cured by drinking or bathing in it. Maybe that's where my family got this water, she thought.

As she grew up, Marie had fewer bumps and bruises. But her tender heart was easily hurt. Schoolyard taunts, slights, unkind words. Such insults made Marie sad.

Seeing this, her mother would bring out the cruet, sprinkle water on Marie's chest and place her hand over her daughter's heart.

"The sacred heals us," she would say.

And Marie would feel better.

When she became a teenager, though, her heartaches got worse. Mean girls and immature boys sent Marie home in tears.

Her mother was always waiting, her blue cruet close at hand.

Years later, Marie had children of her own. They too experienced bumps and bruises.

"Mama, may I borrow your holy water?"

"Of course."

"Mama, you said someday you'd tell me what makes this water holy."

"Yes, I did, and I suppose it's time you know. Marie, there's nothing special about the water in this cruet. It's true that it originally came from France. But that water was used up long ago. I've refilled it from our tap, just as my mother did and her mother before her. It is holy water. But what makes it holy comes only after I've sprinkled it on your body. It is you who make the water holy."

Marie was stunned.

"Mama, why didn't you tell me this before? Why did you keep it a secret?"

"When we're young, we believe God is out there," she said, outstretching her hands. "This is true. It's how we begin to learn about the divine. But in time, we come to understand God also lives within us, that we ourselves are sacred. This is a deeper truth, and it takes time for us to grasp it. Now you know. I hope you'll share this with your children one day."

"I will, Mama."

"But not too soon," she said, handing Marie the cruet.

"Yes," Marie said, kissing her mother's cheek. "Not too soon."

## Unintentional

Elise poured herself a glass of Chardonnay and, as she did nearly every Friday evening, ordered a small pizza for delivery.

How she wished she had someone to share it with. Elise had tried hard for years to find someone. Dating sites, church groups, happy hours, taking a bus to work, volunteering, taking classes, joining a gym, even becoming a "regular" at a coffee shop. But nothing worked. Now 35, Elise was still single.

Not that she heard her "biological clock ticking," though she would welcome being a mother. What she really wanted, though, was a lover. Not for the sex, although she would welcome that too. But for the intimacy, someone with whom she could share her heart.

Elise hadn't found Mr. Right, but she kept her eyes open for any contenders. That's partly why she ordered pizzas on Friday nights. Maybe her lover would appear in the form of a dashing pizza delivery guy. Alas, tonight's potential candidate wasn't shaving yet.

Elise poured another glass of wine, grabbed a slice of pizza and settled in for a movie. What to watch tonight? She'd seen every rom-com on Netflix and couldn't take another one anyway. She picked a documentary about five communities where people live extraordinarily long and vibrant lives. But she fell asleep before it was over.

The following morning, Elise went to a nearby coffee shop where she'd become a regular. On Saturdays, she always got there early, when it wasn't yet crowded. She usually picked a small table in the corner from which she could see all the other customers. All the other prospects.

But by the end of every Saturday morning, Elise was one of the last customers left, and she hadn't met or even spotted any prospects. Maybe she'd seen too many rom-coms, but she kept expecting some handsome guy to approach her table and say, "Would you mind some company?"

This Saturday, though, she'd slept in. Maybe it was that second glass of wine. At any rate, she didn't get to the coffee shop until mid-morning. By then, the place was packed.

Elise had never gotten a coffee to go but, standing in the long line, she considered it. She didn't see an open table. Nor did she see any tables where guys were sitting alone.

But maybe the early morning coffee drinkers will be leaving soon, she thought. She went ahead and ordered her usual latte in a ceramic mug.

By the time it was ready, though, the place was still full. Standing near the door, Elise looked around, hoping someone would leave but also ready to pour her latte into a paper cup.

"You're welcome to share my table," someone said.

Elise looked over. Right next to her stood a pleasant-looking young man. He was standing alone at a tall table with no chairs. Elise hadn't even noticed that table before.

## The Fault, Dear Brutus

As I watched the final election returns, I felt sick. We had elected a madman to lead our country — yet again.

As I thought about what this would mean for the next four years, I couldn't take it. I turned off the TV and went to bed.

When I got downstairs in the morning, my wife was sitting at the kitchen table, sipping her coffee. Her laptop was open.

"How long did you stay up last night?" she said.

"Too long."

"Come here."

I stepped over. She wrapped her arms around my waist and gave me a hug.

"It'll be okay," she said.

"I'm not sure."

"What's wrong?"

"I don't know. I guess I'm afraid."

"Of what?" she said.

"Of what's become of us."

"You mean what *will* become of us."

"No. What's already become of us that something like this could happen."

"Not us," she said. "We didn't vote for him."

"I guess you're right. I mean them."

"Who?"

"You know, all those idiots who voted for him."

"Now wait a minute, Jim. We both know a lot of people who voted for him, my dad included."

"I didn't mean your dad."

"But Dad *did* vote for him. So did Caroline."

"Don't remind me. Where did I go wrong?"

"Jim!"

"Sorry. It's just ..."

"Just what?"

"It's just that it doesn't make any sense. How could anyone ever vote for a man like that?"

"Our country is very divided."

"It's more than divided, Deb. It's toxic."

"Toxic?"

"Yeah. We're at each other's throats anymore."

"Maybe so. But our elections have always been contentious."

"Not like this. And I'm not talking about just elections. People are no longer civil on a good day."

"Who are you talking about?"

I was getting frustrated that my own wife didn't seem more sympathetic.

"Everybody," I said, buttering my toast.

"Honey, that's just not true. We know a lot of good people, people who are respectful."

"Well, I wish they'd go into politics."

She stared out the window and said nothing.

"I just wish we had leaders we could look up to," I said.

"Like who, Jim? We haven't had a President you've liked since I've known you."

She had a point.

"Well, there was a time when I wasn't afraid our democracy might crash and burn," I said.

"I get it. I'm worried too. Do you know the League of Women Voters had to pay people to work the polls yesterday? That's never happened before."

"Is that legal?"

"I don't know. But what are we going to do if people can't vote?"

"I guess you're right."

"You used to work the polls," she said softly.

"Yeah."

"Why don't you anymore?"

"I don't know."

"And you were so active with the Kiwanis."

Again, she had a point.

"Jim, I'm sorry. I'm not trying to pick a fight or blame you for anything. I used to be more involved too. Now we just sit here all day, online. We take Zoom meetings. We never go out. We hardly see our friends anymore."

"Yeah. We've become insular. Maybe we're all so divided these days because we don't really know each other anymore."

She looked sad.

"Why don't we go to dinner tonight?" I said.

"It's supposed to rain."

"We can get takeout. I can pick it up."

"Okay," she said, turning to her laptop.

I popped in a coffee cartridge and brewed myself another cup.

"Have a good —" I said, about to wish her a good morning, but she wasn't paying attention.

"Huh?" she said, her gazed fixed on her screen.

"We've become like them," I said.

"What?" she said, looking up with a faint smile.

"Never mind," I said, turning around and heading upstairs for a meeting.

## The Conversation

Andrew awoke and, for the first time in a long time, felt no pain. In fact, he couldn't feel his body at all. He opened his eyes and looked down, but his body wasn't there.

He looked around. Everything was white. Nothing had form. This isn't hospice, he thought.

He heard a voice.

"Hello, Andrew."

The voice was warm. It was neither male nor female. He couldn't place it, yet it seemed familiar.

"Hello?" Andrew said.

Then he realized the owner of the voice was very close, though Andrew could see no one.

"Where am I?" he said.

"Where you've always been."

"But I don't know this place."

"You did once, before you were born. You lived a long life. At first, it can be hard to remember."

"Who are you?"

"You know me. You've always known me."

"Refresh my memory."

"Ha, ha."

"I'm serious."

"I know. But you do make me laugh."

"That's good. At least I hope it is."

"It's very good. When you laugh, you put aside your cares. I love that."

"But I worried a lot."

"A whole lot."

"Did you still love me then?"

"I've always loved you."

"Can I ask you something?"

"Sure."

"How did I do?"

"Wonderfully."

"Come on. Really."

"You did the best you could."

"But I could have done better."

"What do you mean?"

"I wasn't a great father. I wasn't a great husband."

"Why do you say that?"

"Well, I wasn't very dutiful."

"Is that what it means to be a good father or a good husband?"

"But I should have been there more."

"You loved them, and they loved you. That is enough."

"Really?"

"Yes."

"But I haven't always been faithful."

"I know."

"Oh, yeah," Andrew said, feeling a bit self-conscious, even though he could no longer see himself.

"You think you failed, but I've always been with you, and I would never let you fail."

"I didn't achieve much, though."

"Did you use your talent?"

"I tried."

"That too is enough."

"Well, I drank too much."

"Yes, you did."

"And I didn't go to church much."

"I noticed."

"I shot a bird with a BB gun when I was a kid."

"I know."

"I killed the poor thing!"

"I know. I wept."

"I'm sorry. That was wrong."

"You were learning. Besides, I forgave you."

Andrew thought for a moment.

"You mean none of the bad things I did in my life really mattered?"

"How did those things make you feel?"

"Bad."

"Why?"

"Well, I guess I felt I had disappointed ... you know."

"God?"

"Yeah."

"But, Andrew, you are one with God."

"I am now."

"You always have been."

"Really?"

"Yes."

"I wish I'd known that."

"You did."

"When?"

"Whenever you loved someone or felt loved."

"Those were good moments."

"And they were just glimpses of what's to come."

"You mean there's more than this?"

"Oh, yes. This has just been a conversation to get reacquainted. Would you like to see the rest?"

"Yeah."

"Let me show you."

## The Garden

The old man raised the mattock high and brought it down hard into the encrusted earth. His back hurt and his arms trembled, but he had to go on.

Fifty years earlier, he had broken up this patch of land in their backyard for her. For nearly 50 years, she planted and tended flowers here. Aside from her, that garden was the most beautiful thing he had ever seen.

But the land had lain fallow for three years now, while he tended to her. He simply had to restore her garden. It was his only way to see her again.

## See for Yourself

"Cars," said five-year-old Lochan as his father kissed him goodbye.

"Cars?" his father said, watching as the boy, blind since birth, struggled to find his mouth with his cereal spoon.

"Cars," Lochan said again.

"What do you mean?"

"Cars," Lochan mumbled with a mouthful of Apple Jacks.

"Okay, cars," his father said with a smile. "I'll see you all tonight."

As his father closed the door to the garage behind him, his mother said, "Lochan, honey, finish your breakfast. You'll be late for school."

About an hour later, Lochan's father returned home. Saying nothing, he walked into the family room, sat down on the sofa and stared blankly at the fireplace.

"Bob?" his wife said. "Are you okay?"

"There was a nine-car pileup on 70," he said. "It happened right in front of me. I was almost in it. I hit my brakes just in time."

"Oh, Bob," she said, wrapping her arms around him. "How awful. I'm so glad you're okay."

"Cars," he said.

She looked puzzled.

"I've been worried about the way people drive lately. Remember? I even mentioned it at dinner last night. After Lochan said that this morning, I had cars on my mind. I stayed in the right lane and drove slow. Thank God I did."

Then he turned to her and said, "That boy has a gift."

Word got around about Lochan's gift. People came to him as if he were an oracle. He would listen to their questions and problems, then say something simple. People left in awe, as if some great, hidden truth had been revealed to them.

Maybe it was his disability, which was off-putting for children, especially in those days, or his mysterious reputation as a fortune teller. But sadly Lochan had no close friends growing up.

After high school, he got a job as a customer service representative. It was a job he could do from home.

When his sister moved out, Lochan was often alone. He cooked for himself. He listened to music, audiobooks and news. He walked on a treadmill.

Years later, when his father died, his mother sold their house and moved to a retirement center. Lochan went with her. When she died, he stayed.

A kind aide named Maddie befriended Lochan. She'd seen him sitting alone and made an effort to talk with him. So many people had come to Lochan for advice over the years, but few had ever really talked with him.

One day, Maddie asked Lochan about his "gift."

"That's what my parents called it," he said.

"Well, isn't it?"

"Not really."

"What do you mean?"

"When I was a kid, sometimes I would hear a word and say it for no particular reason. People thought I knew something they didn't, maybe because I'm blind. Anyway, they started coming to me with questions. In their questions, I could always hear their answers. I don't have a gift, Maddie. All I've done is help people see for themselves what they already know."

## Perfect Communion

Crouched over, leaning heavily on his cane, Jack Lohman shuffled behind the last row of pews until he reached the center aisle of the church. These days he sat at the end of the last pew in case he needed to go to the bathroom during Mass. He wanted to be the last in line for Communion anyway so he wouldn't hold anyone up.

Today he was there for the funeral of his old friend, Al. Eight decades earlier, they'd gone to grade school together right next door. Now as Jack got in line for Communion, he eyed Al's casket up ahead.

He'd been in this church for the funerals of many friends in recent years. This morning, it was packed. Al was beloved.

As he shambled forward, Jack also thought of the funerals there for his wife and, years earlier, their son. Their presence had filled him with joy. Their absence still filled him with sorrow.

Looking up at the sanctuary, he remembered his daughter standing there, looking radiant in her wedding gown.

And there was the marble baptismal font, where his children had been baptized and he himself had been baptized so long ago.

Jack spotted a teenager in line ahead of him and thought of the special evening when he, as a teen, knelt at this Communion rail, and the Archbishop confirmed him.

Then he saw a young boy and remembered the excitement of making his very first Communion, not far from where he now stood.

Now all those who had been in line ahead of Jack had received Communion and returned to their seats. Jack stood alone in the aisle, beside the casket. He rested his palm on the linen pall draped over it and said a silent, final farewell.

Looking at the priest, patiently awaiting his last communicant, Jack felt a strange sensation, as if he were rising. Suddenly, he was hovering above the entire congregation.

Jack looked down at the casket. The lid was now gone, and inside lay not his friend, but Jack himself. And yet Jack was not afraid. On the contrary, he felt safe and warm, like a newborn in its mother's arms. As he looked around, he realized everyone in the church was there for him. He could feel their affection.

Then Jack was gathered in by all his loved ones, everyone he had ever known and a benevolent presence he had felt all his life. He was one with all of them and all things. He was, at last, in perfect Communion.

## History Lesson

For 75 years, David Moore thought about a letter he had written when he was 10 years old.

He wrote it in the fourth grade as a school assignment. His teacher, Mrs. Chamberlain, was trying to help her students understand history — specifically, how our perspective on current events changes over time and how our perspective, not just the events themselves, becomes what we know as history.

To try to bring this lesson home, she had her students write letters to themselves about something that was happening in their lives and what it meant to them. She wanted them to then put the letter away and read it years in the future.

"What you see a certain way today may take on a completely different meaning years from now," she said. "You'll see."

David chose to write about his greatest fear at that moment in his life. His parents were divorcing. He didn't know why, but he remembered blaming his mother.

Years later, just before David left for college, his mom told him his father had beat her. He wouldn't stop, she said. She couldn't take it any longer and feared for the safety of her children. So she left him and filed for divorce.

David was stunned.

"Why didn't you tell me, Mom?"

"I didn't want you to hate your father. But I'm telling you now, before you go out into the world. I want you to promise me you'll always treat everyone with respect. I want you to promise me you'll never hit a woman."

"Oh, Mom. I promise."

They were both crying, and they held each other a long time.

Over the years, David looked for his letter but could never find it. Now he and his wife Sandy were moving out of their house and into a retirement community.

They'd lived in their house for 50 years, and deciding what to keep and what to give away was a monumental task. Fortunately, their children, Brian and Kimberly, and their spouses, Nicole and Matt, were a big help.

One day, Kimberly came up from the basement holding an envelope.

"Here, Dad," she said, handing it to him. "I found this on the bottom a box. It's got your name on it."

David recognized his youthful handwriting, and his mind raced back to that school assignment. With shaking hands, he carefully opened the envelope, unfolded the letter inside and read it.

*December 10, 1958*

*Dear David,*

*Today I found out Mom and Dad are going to get a divorce. That means they won't be married anymore.*

*Mom told me. She didn't say why they're getting a divorce, only that their marriage "wasn't working" and, from now on, Carol, Joe and I will live with her.*

*Mom says she still loves Dad. But if that's true, then why are they getting a divorce?*

*I don't think Mom is telling the truth. It seems like she's hiding something. Dad has always been good to me, but she threw him out, and now I can't talk to him. I think this might be Mom's fault.*

*Mrs. Chamberlain says we should read these letters years from now, that how we see something today will change over time. All I know is that my parents are getting a divorce, and I don't trust my mom anymore. And I don't care what Mrs. Chamberlain says, that's not going to change.*

*I hope we'll all be OK.*

*Signed,*

*David Moore*

David's eyes welled with tears.

"Are you okay?" Sandy said.

"Yeah," he said, wiping his eyes.

Then he asked everyone to have a seat in the family room. He told them about his school assignment and what Mrs. Chamberlain had said about history unfolding over time. Then he read his letter out loud.

"Oh, Dad," Kimberly said. "That must have been such a hard time for you."

"It was," David said. "But there's much more to the story."

"There is?" Sandy said.

"Yes, and it's something I haven't told any of you."

Nobody said anything. Nobody knew what to say.

Then he told them what his mother had told him all those years ago and the promise he made to her.

"Oh, honey," Sandy said, putting her arm around him.

"I'm sorry I didn't tell you," David said. "It was just too painful. I was ashamed. I was ashamed for my mother."

"But you were true to your word," Sandy said. "You've never hit me."

"Or me," Kimberly said.

"Or me," said Brian.

"David, don't you remember?" Sandy said. "Before we were married, you told me you would never hit me and made me promise we would never hit our children."

David nodded.

Kimberly and Brian looked at their spouses.

"Dad," Kimberly said, "Mom told us that, and Matt and I made the same promise to each other before we got married. We told our kids, and they and their spouses made the same promise to each other too."

"Same with us and our kids," Brian said, taking Nicole's hand.

David looked at them all and smiled. He realized his mother's suffering and the pain and shame he had felt as a boy had been transformed into relationships based on respect, down through the generations.

It was all now part of his family's history, which had taken years to unfold and was still unfolding. Mrs. Chamberlain was right, David thought.

## Play

"We don't stop playing because we grow old. We grow old because we stop playing."

— George Bernard Shaw

"Where to?" he asked his granddaughter Lucy as they stepped off the merry-go-round.

"Roller coaster!"

"That one?" he said, pointing to the kiddie coaster.

"No, Poppy. The big one!"

"Are you sure you're ready for that?"

"Yes," Lucy said, rolling her eyes. "I'm eight!"

"Okay."

When his kids were growing up, he'd taken them on the big coaster countless times. But that was 25 years ago. The last time he rode this coaster it made him sick, and he swore he'd never ride it again.

Now he and Lucy were heading for that very coaster. He'd begun taking her to this amusement park once a summer. Until now, she'd been content with the kiddie rides. But Lucy was growing up. She was adventurous and full of energy. As they got in line, she bounced on the balls of her feet with excitement.

"Do you love this ride, Poppy?"

"I used to. I haven't ridden it in a long time."

"Why?"

He thought for a moment. He didn't want to scare her.

"Because I haven't been out of kiddie land for years."

That was true. But it was also true that he just wasn't up to riding the bigger coasters anymore.

"This is going to be so fun!" Lucy said with a big smile.

She looks so much like her mother as a girl, he thought. That seemed so long ago, before his life became so serious, when he still took time to play. A lifetime ago.

Now they were at the front of the line. Watching the coaster glide toward them, he felt like baling out. But as it came to a stop and the aluminum gates swung open, Lucy said, "Come on, Poppy!" and he followed her into their car.

He slid in beside her and helped her with her seatbelt before buckling his own. Then he lowered the safety bar. Too late to turn back now.

A ride attendant made her way along the cars, tugging on the bars to make sure they were secure.

"All clear," someone said over the loudspeaker.

The coaster took off slowly. It snaked around a bend, then began climbing the big first hill. Click, click, click. He held tight to the safety bar. His heart was pounding. His forehead was beaded with sweat.

"How high will we go, Poppy?"

He looked over at his granddaughter. Now she looked worried. She's too young to worry, he thought. Life will get serious soon enough.

He held out his hand. She took it and squeezed it tight.

"Everything will be okay, Lu," he said with a smile.

When they reached the top, he let out a whoop, like he used to as a boy. That made Lucy laugh. They held hands and screamed in delight the rest of the way.

As they rolled into the station, Lucy said, "Let's go again, Poppy!"

"Okay," he said, still holding her small hand.

# Acknowledgments

I want to thank my wife Liz, Libby Belle, Kathy Kennedy and Patti Normile for all their help and encouragement.

I also want to extend grateful acknowledgment to the editors of *Cantos, Literary Yard, The Seattle Star, Waves of Words, Bright Flash Literary Review* and *Friday Flash Fiction*, the literary magazines where the original versions of some of these stories appeared.

Don Tassone

Made in United States
North Haven, CT
07 July 2024